Exponential Ten

CHRIS LEVICK

authorHOUSE

AuthorHouse™ UK
1663 Liberty Drive
Bloomington, IN 47403 USA
www.authorhouse.co.uk
Phone: UK TFN: 0800 0148641 (Toll Free inside the UK)
        UK Local: (02) 0369 56322 (+44 20 3695 6322 from outside the UK)

Published by AuthorHouse 07/11/2022

ISBN: 978-1-7283-7423-9 (sc)
ISBN: 978-1-7283-7422-2 (e)

CHAPTER 1

Eighteen years ago
22 May 2002, 2200 hours
Special Forces Operations
Afghanistan

The Chinook CH-47F, the world's fastest military helicopter, weighing 33,000 pounds, thundered and thudded its way high over the desert in a north-westerly direction from its base in Kandahar. Its cargo consisted of two Land Rover British Army vehicles, specially adapted to driving over the dunes, and four special duties personnel.

As it approached the mountains south of Kabul, it changed course to a more westerly direction to confuse any attempt to interpret its destination and started to gain height. It cut through the air with its twin-engine, tandem-rotor, bone-shaking chopping action and flew up into the mountainous valleys and through unoccupied passes, a display of high experience and nerve in the dark from the pilots who would deliver their load twenty clicks from the target.

The mission was to safely extract Major Newton, Private Steve Shaw, and two Afghanistan interpreters who had gone missing thirty-two hours earlier at a position 480 klicks northeast of Kandahar at 1600 hours, 21 May. A sting operation by the Taliban had abducted a British officer in order to obtain British military information. Past abductees had never come back alive. Major Newton had been lured into a meet with an informer, who had previously passed on good information. He looked as if he could give intel about the location of the local Taliban headquarters.

Major Newton had not arranged any kind of backup, as he considered the informant to be trusted. They had arrived near the pre arranged location. As they made their way down a channel beside the wall to the abandoned property, Major Newton realised the two interpreters had fallen behind. He turned round to hurry them along so they could stay in one group for more safety. Private Shaw had arrived ahead of them. He had decided, unwisely, as it turned out, to enter the building on his own. As Private Shaw turned the corner through a door opening into the yard, he was seized and had his throat sliced through, after which he was dragged to one side and thrown into the building. Major Newton walked straight into the ambush. He and the interpreters had their hands taped together and were bundled into the backs of three vehicles, which had sped off from their rendezvous. Private Shaw was already dead. His body was never recovered.

Clear skies and low cloud density enabled the movement of enemy vehicles travelling north three hundred miles to a village location caught on satellite via Government Communications Headquarters (GCHQ) in the United Kingdom. A rescue party was immediately sent under the command of Sergeant Simon Knight, nicknamed Darkly (SBS seconded to special duties under SAS.) The silent, dark, and cold desert night sent a shiver through Knight's toned body, even though sweat was dripping from his brown hair onto his collar. Every few steps, he stopped and listened to the noises of the desert and this eerily unoccupied village. It was deathly quiet. He kept looking left and right up the alleyways, peering through even the dirtiest window, looking up onto every roof and continuously searching for something out of place. His torch caught sight of footprints in the dust. On closer inspection, possibly for drag marks too. Darkly's senses were now on high alert.

As he passed an old blue door on his right, it was wrenched open with a sharp crack, making him stop short. Sergeant Simon Knight had less than a second to make up his mind to crouch down, move back, or jump into the light that shined out from the small earthen-floored room and beyond. He chose the latter. The light led his eyes through a narrow opening to these single-story houses.

He jumped into the shining light from the room, which was immediately blocked out by what he saw in front of him, a larger-than-average Afghanistan fighter. Darkly was well over six feet, and this fella was taller still, with a Kalashnikov AK-47 slung over one shoulder and spare ammunition rounds draped over both shoulders. The Afghan soldier's eyes went wide with surprise as he looked up to see the butt of Darkly's rifle connect with his chin. The big guy went straight down. Darkly had to step over him to see into the front room. He clearly saw Major Newton taped to a chair. He had two black eyes and blood coming from his right ear, and his head had been slumped onto his chest. His first impression was he had been worked over quite thoroughly. At the noise of the intrusion, Newton looked up. A guard, who was about to take a red-hot poker out of a fire blazing under an oven on the far wall, turned around towards Darkly. There was another guard sitting to the right; He double-tapped the poker man and then did the same to the other guard in the chair. Four strides later, he was across the room, his knife out, slashing Newton free while looking around for any more enemy operatives.

"Where have you been? Any later, and they would have had my eyes out, for Christ's sake. There's three more in the far room."

"OK, we're here now. Make your way to the street. Our unit's out there."

Darkly took out a flashbang and fired one round into the locking mechanism of the door where Newton had pointed. He took two strides forward, smashed the door open with his foot, and threw the flashbang into the room, closing the door while he waited for the bang. It went off within a second. The flash would have completely blinded anyone in its proximity, and the deafening noise would disorientate everyone in the room. Thick smoke followed the bright light. He waited no longer before leaping into the room.

He went down on one knee in a low crouch on the floor of the darkened room. He immediately saw the two interpreters, whom they

3

had also come to rescue. They were strung up by their ankles and covered in blood and looked to be in a bad way. He double-tapped the two guards to the left and swung around to take out the guard on the right. The guard was obviously disorientated; however, he continued to raise his weapon in Darkly's direction. In that split second, Darkly thought this was going to be close, even though the guy was shaking. At that same moment, there was the unmistakable rattle of a Browning over his shoulder and a plume of blood that looped up the wall and up onto the ceiling. Bits of plaster spat into the room, and the guard hit the ground.

"That's all the bastards in the house," Darkly heard Corporal Beck shout behind him. He went forward and cut the two interpreters down. No time for dressings or any first aid; they had to get out as fast as they could. Knight knew his team had heard the radio messages and would come to help in this otherwise uninhabited and desolate little village.

As they made the street one interpreter each in a fireman's lift, they were met by their two colleagues. Corporal Beck was immediately on his radio, calling in the Chinook to their rendezvous point. One of the others, Lance Corporal Dick Williams, took the interpreter who was in the worst medical condition. Newton, himself was kneeling beng violently sick on the ground, he had started to shake. He had been badly hit and beaten, and they would have tortured him if allowed to carry on using the red-hot poker. He knew it could have been one eye or both. The second interpreter was moaning in the ground.

The Taliban were a murderous enemy. The year before, they had captured a soldier, tied him to four stakes in the ground, and started the torture by cutting off his eyelids. The poor boy had to watch everything they did to him. Then over two days, they skinned him alive, leaving him in the sun uncovered with a small amount of water—just enough, SAS mates reckoned, to keep him alive long enough so they could hear his screams, which could be heard ten miles away during the two nights it took him to die.

The group now was made up of Major Peter Newton, Sergeant

Simon Knight (Darkly) in command, Corporal Tom Beck, Lance Corporal Dick Williams, and Private Geoff Bradley. They made their way as quickly as possible towards their Land Rovers. As they came around the corner of the last house, shots rang out from their two-o'clock position at about seventy yards. The shots hit the ground all wide of the mark, kicking up grass and dust, and to their left, the shots imbedded into some rocks about four feet high and ten feet long. They took cover behind the rocks to their left and put the two interpreters against the back. After a quick discussion, Darkly and Tom Beck took off as fast as they could in opposite directions to the gunfire and disappeared behind a line of houses.

As they separated to create a wide arc to encircle their enemy, Darkly stumbled over the a body which lay in his path, amid the dark, the dust and intertwined legs. He glanced down at the horizontal pupils of a goat. He hatched a plan that might confuse their enemy— if he could get the goat to traverse a clearing about thirty yards ahead. He used the tape he had taken off Peter Newton when he had released him and wound it around the snout of the goat, which stopped it from bleating. It didn't, however, stop it from struggling and kicking as it tried to get free. He led the unhappy grunting animal in a circle to the right.

He knew Beck had seen what had happened and had not come back. Fearing he could break cover and give his position away, both of them would take a wide circle, knowing the two who had let off the rounds would think Darkly's group would try to escape as fast as they could or would they come back to find them? The former was the most likely, Darkly and his colleague, who were now out of sight of one another, prepared their weapons. Darkly whipped the tape from around the goat's snout and gave the unhappy animal a sharp crack between its back legs, connecting with its gonads, which made it fly across the ground. Three shots rang out, and on the third, the big guy Darkly had clubbed earlier fell to the ground, sporting a 5.56 mm hole in the middle of his forehead. At the same moment, two shots took the second Taliban fighter's lights out. Darkly was glad to see that the poor old goat had not been hit and had scampered off into the darkness and chill of the mountains. Darkly and Beck ran over to ensure were both dead, then doubled back to where the main group were waiting.

Out of breath and with sweat running down their faces, they made good time back to meet up with their team and locate the two Land Rovers. They agreed to travel in convoy with Darkly and Private Geoff Bradley in the lead vehicle. This was followed by Major Peter Newton, Corporal Tom Beck (Trickle), Lance Corporal Dick Williams, and the two interpreters in the back of the second Land Rover on makeshift beds, located on either side of the turret for the Vickers gun. Private Beck travelled in the very back of this Land Rover, doing his best to keep the two injured men as comfortable as possible. The worse of the two, whose tongue had been cut off three inches from its tip and had low blood pressure, an increased heart rate, and rapid breathing, which they couldn't reduce, and likely suffering from abdominal bleeding due to the beatings, could only be saved by surgery back at basecamp. They reasoned he might not make the journey.

They didn't want to draw attention to themselves, so they kept away from main routes and headed down from the mountainous region, keeping to small lanes and dried-up riverbeds towards their rendezvous with the Chinook. The terrain was appalling for the two interpreters, who were flung about and bumped around continuously, grunting and moaning from the discomfort of their injuries. They had been savagely beaten and tortured, but all the others could do was look at each other with weariness, knowing this journey had to be taken this way, as the alternative would have put them all in too much danger.

They arrived at their rendezview and within ten minutes heard the unmistakable twin thump-thump-thump-thump of the Chinook as it beat and shook the ground. Amid a storm of sand and small pebbles, it landed and immediately released the cargo bay door. As soon as it hit the ground, a figure stood to one side and waved them through to drive straight up and into the bay itself. As soon as the second Land Rover came to a halt and while the cargo bay door was reclosing, the Chinook lifted into the air, and they were away to base camp.

The group arrived back at Kandahar base camp, and as predicted even immediate medical help on the flight could not save the life of the interpreter whose tongue had been cut, and the loss of private Shaw . A sad end to an otherwise successful rescue mission conducted by Sergeant Simon Knight.

Major Newton resigned his commission at the end of that tour and went on to become a Member of Parliament. He had not been a popular Rupert, and there was the obvious talk as to whether he might have been pushed, a regular occurrence among Ruperts who didn't make the grade. This was all too obvious to the lower ranks.

CHAPTER 2

Present Day
10 Downing Street

Simon Knight stayed on in the SBS for three more years in the navy and subsequently with Special Forces. It had been good for him, and it was with sad feelings that he finally decided to move on. He had left the navy following twenty-four years of distinguished service. He stayed with the home office and worked under Metropolitan Police Service security at Number Ten Downing Street. He had welcomed the change and enjoyed the work. He rose through the ranks and had been promoted to take command of the ex-military and trained staff and was in overall control of Number Ten Downing Street security and the movements of the prime minister.

The red phone buzzed, and Darkly picked it up, knowing it was the PM on the other end.

The British prime minister had arrived on the crest of a wave of resentment by the voters, sick of years of over-taxation and government overspending. The treasury was crumbling and in need of funds. The spending budget of the previous government had been huge, and there was little left. Brett Caddick was a sensible candidate who was well-liked, even by those among the opposition. He had worked hard at his state school. Both his parents were teachers, which helped with his academic aspirations.

He had studied biological sciences at Manchester University, gaining an MSc, which allowed him to satiate his actual interest:

ornithology. Following his time at Manchester, he spent two years in the Scottish Islands, doing research. He hadn't wanted to go into academia or business, so a chance position in the Department of Agriculture took his interest. He had to be in London and lived in a rented longboat on the Thames with a university friend. His friend had suggested they go along to a local political meeting, mainly to meet girls their own age. This is where he met Margo and became interested in politics.

Margo was a social worker, and they found they had a lot in common. Brett joined the local party and was elected to the district council. He became deputy leader within three years and found himself pushed forward to stand for the Member of Parliament for that borough in London when it became vacant. Brett had never envisaged himself as an MP. He didn't want to displease party members when they had put him forward and was shocked to find he had become their representative when he was duly elected. He had a pleasant nature and became known as a decent and honest parliamentarian who persevered and got things done. Over the next five years, he and Margo married, enabling him to buy a house south of the river. Margo gave birth to two children, which made their lives complete. He became party leader by default, simply because he was the last man standing, as he liked to explain.

Brett Caddick had a complicated relationship with the American president. Brett, who could hold his own intellectually also, often felt bullied and manipulated by Ethan Miller. They had just endured one of Ethan's "listen to me and shut up and do what I say" telephone conversations, which centred on climate change and its consequences, leaving Brett Caddick feeling sick in the stomach.

He was a decent man caught in the moment, Darkly thought. In his sixties, losing his hair, and of medium height, he wasn't going to pull the skin off a rice pudding as a pioneer, but he was easier than most to get along with and much better than the deputy PM, with whom Darkly had served, even saving his life. The deputy PM was one Peter Newton.

Darkly arrived at the PM's office and knocked on the substantial door. He entered after the PM called out to come in. The Prime Minister motioned Darkly to one of the two comfortable armchairs he liked to use for intimate chats. Over the next fifteen minutes, Brett Caddick told him how the US president had told him that he had been the first person to be informed that there was to be a mid-Atlantic meeting, completely confidential and held on an American aircraft carrier just south of Greenland. Only friendly nuclear-powered countries would be invited. Darkly was not to speak to anyone about it, except that he would go first and alone in a Tornado F-35—departure 0700 hours tomorrow morning, journey time fifty-three minutes. He would be picked up from home at 0600 hours by a RAF staff car. His brief was to check out security onboard USS *George Bush*, the biggest of the eight American aircraft carriers positioned in the North Atlantic.

"Oh, yes, before I forget, there is a guy called Matt Drayson from M15 who wants you in the small office on the second floor when I've finished with you."

"OK, sir. I'll nip up there straight away."

Darkly went out of the office and up the stairs to the second floor, knocking on the door of the small office.

"Come in, come in."

Matt Drayson was young, keen, and green. Not tall, although no one came up to Darkly's height. Probably his first field job, he guessed. He had got up out of the chair to shake Darkly's hand.

"We have a new little device we would like you to trial. We think it is undetectable. It's a new listening device, which is impossible to detect at the present time. You need to squeeze it out of a tube. It is transparent and sets in one minute. Try to find a joint under a piece of furniture so you can find it again easily. As soon as it sets, it records every sound for twenty-four hours. It has a silicon base and will therefore stick to most things. It will not show up on any known detection devices. We have put it into the arm of a pair of reading spectacles, as we were able to access your lens requirement."

Drayson handed him a pair of normal reading glasses, and on the right-hand arm, Darkly could feel the sac at the end. He put them on and smiled as they allowed him to focus normally.

"No one knows you're trialling this for us, not even the PM. When you have retrieved the strip and placed it in the glasses case, it will travel quite well enough in your pocket. Any questions so far?"

"No, I'm fine so far. Only one thing: Does it smell before it sets?"

"That's the trick: no smell whatsoever. Neat, eh? When you get back, phone me, and we can see what it picks up. Just remember: this is totally secret. Here's my card."

CHAPTER 3

The mobile the president of the United States of America kept for a very few important people across the world bleeped out its signal for an incoming call. Ethan Miller looked around his Oval Office. There were two people over on the far side. He nodded at them and cocked his head to the right. They left the room.

"Hi. Ethan Miller speaking. Feel free to talk."

"Peter Newton, Deputy Prime Minister United Kingdom, speaking, sir."

"Yeah, right. Gotya, Peter. You're the SAS guy who wants to be PM? Impressed my wife."

"Yes, that's correct. I mean, sorry, sir, not about your wife."

"OK, calm down. That's fine, Peter. Have you got good news for me?"

"Yes, I managed to get the Oxford paper 'Catastrophic Climatic Changes' and have been able to take bits out and added the paragraph you asked to be included."

"Perfect. I'm organising the Atlantic meeting this week, so it's come at the right time. What do you want me to do with your PM, the man who won't play my game?"

"Quite so. I'm happy to be of service, Ethan. If you can make him look stupid in front of the other leaders and maybe to voice the fact that Brett Caddick had known all about your scheme to become the only large manufacturer nation in the world."

"OK, buddy. It's great to be batting on the same team together. You scratch my back and I'll scratch yours." He closed the call.

Ethan Miller had a malevolent look of satisfaction on his crooked face. He was now able to use the distinguished paper from Oxford, England, which Peter Newton had doctored for him, to back up his untrue predictions on climate change to bend the world to his demands, and to help him, he was using this little weasel, who, if he did become prime minister in the UK, would truly be under his thumb.

Later that afternoon, Peter Newton sat opposite the head of MI5, William Hassop-Greene.

William Hassop-Greene said, "So, you want me to discredit our current prime minister and do all I'm asked by you. On top of that, you want me to hound Simon Knight, removing him, if necessary, to eliminate any obstacles to you taking over as prime minister. Frankly, Peter, ever since our time together at Charnhouse, I would never have imagined you to come up with such a selfish and unethical plot, and you expect my help?"

"It's like this, William. When you were in the lower and Upper Sixth, I was in the next study to you, as you may remember. I saw the succession of fags you abused. Innocent young boys. You weren't happy, like the rest of us, to enjoy a bit of normal fagging. You had to go one step further and rape them. Don't deny it, because I have personally spoken to three of them—namely Gofrey, Cameron, and Armstrong. I have even been in touch recently."

"You little bastard. You evil turd. You're wizened, conniving, slimy, filthy fucker." He was puce, his words were being spat out of his mouth which was foaming with the fury and panic in his head from this unexpected onslaught to his dignity. Newton had been an unliked slithering turd at Charnhouse, with very few friends. This was an earth-shaker. His own Polo membership, his golf club, the honours list for his work in MI5, his wife, his family—all gone, and down to a half-being like Peter Newton.

Newton held up his hand. "Let me not be the harbinger of completely bad threats, William. I have a solution. When I become prime minister, I would like to amalgamate both MI5 and MI6 into one unit. I would have you running both, and there would be a knighthood at the end of a distinguished career. Does that sound better?"

"Your cunning little rat."

"Do we have a deal then, or do you need more time to think it over?" Hassop-Greene's colour had returned to normal, and his breathing had stopped coming in gulps. He could see that this nasty little rat had him by the hairs up his nose—to rake up the past like that—and he knew Newton should not be anywhere near running the country. However, when there's a door open, take it.

"OK, I'll do what you want. When do we start?"

"I'll email you some misinformation on Caddick, and I'll let you know when to release it. There is also an American meeting with heads of state coming up, and the US president wants a favour from me, which I can give him. It keeps me in the loop and covers our backs."

Peter Newton got up and didn't shake hands with Hassop-Greene, for which the latter was pleased. It was one thing to side with the devil. It was another to make out they were friends. Newton let himself out of the office and made his way towards the lifts, and as he got to the doors, he turned right and took the stairs. The fewer people to see him, the better. If Hassop-Greene's hate had power, it would have thrown Newton through the toughened glass windows, and he would have landed on the pavement outside, dead. Hassop-Greene fumed quietly, calming himself with the knowledge that his future was about to make him a very important person. He became excited just thinking about it.

CHAPTER 4

North Atlantic

As Simon Knight looked over his right shoulder, he could see the USS *George H Bush* aircraft carrier in the dark Atlantic sea half a mile below them. It looked insignificant from up here, and the deck area appeared as a postage stamp, as impossible on which to land as the last totally hectic 48 hours had been for him to navigate. He was shaken alert by the headset jumping into action as the RAF fighter pilot reopened communications with the conning tower on the ship below. As they lost height, the great city of a ship, out here in the middle of an uneasy ocean, looked more and more massive, and they started to line up with the US navy personnel waving his batons and showing them where he wanted them on his deck. They circled and came into the headwind, which would give them the greatest manoeuvrability as they descended the last 300 meters. The deck area still looked impossibly small to him as he watched the long vessel heave and sigh in the huge swell of the North Atlantic.

In no time at all the, Tornado seemed to pitch and roll to the movement of the deck, and after quite a thump, they had landed. The engines, having been switched off, screeched and whined as though punishing the hand that cut their life. The cacophony of activity hit him first, and then, the wind reminded him where he was now and the comfort of the cockpit where the exactness of modern science came together under the controlled calmness of the pilots' genius. It had given him a feeling of wonder and safety.

The canopy opened on a hinge behind him, and Darkly clambered out of the cockpit, feeling his way onto the wheeled ladder which had been placed against the fuselage and locked. As he hit the deck, he looked up to see a very tidy young lady officer coming towards him. She was younger than him, obviously very fit, and had her fair hair up in a neat bun under her cap. She saluted and said, "Hello, sir. Chief Petty Officer Jane Fraser here to escort you to the wardroom. Would you like to follow me, please?"

She took him through the big door leading off the main deck. It thudded behind them. Down below decks, they they traversed the corridors, which seemingly went on for miles, and finally to the wardroom, where the meeting was to take place. Chief Petty Officer Fraser was a graduate, like him, and trying to find a career in a man's world, where they had opened the door to include women. She was brisk in her movement and appeared to be extremely focused. It made up for her medium stature. She gained some height from having her hair up in a bun under her cap. The way she carried herself showed her to be athletic and fit, Darkly couldn't help but notice. He admired women who kept themselves in shape and wanted to get on in life, especially in this male-dominated world of servicemen.

Jane's family came from Montana, which had given her a rural life near the Rocky Mountains. Marjorie, her mother, was a nurse in St Peters Hospital, Broadway Street, in Helena. Robert, her dad, worked for a pump maintenance company, and he doted on his daughter. She had a twin brother, Darren, to whom she was dedicated. Darren had beaten Jane into the world by forty-five minutes, and he always saw this as his excuse to look after her at all times and make sure she was OK. They had been brought up in the Christian faith, and the whole family were busily involved in the local community. Robert's father had fought in the South Pacific against the Japanese in World War Two, and although he had an extremely hard time, his service to their country had always impressed his grandchildren.

Jane had started dating Judd Musgrove in her ninth-grade year. He was the captain of the basketball team and a year older than Jane. Her parents approved, as they knew Judd's parents from their church.

Once Judd had gone off to college, however, he never contacted Jane again, and it nearly broke her heart. She had Darren, her family, and a close network of school buddies to give her the comfort she needed. It did, however, teach her never to trust men again in general.

Jane and her brother had both completed their National Merit Scholarships, and when Darren chose to enter the US Air Force, Jane decided the US Navy was her choice. The jolt from relocating from small-town Montana to the largest navy in the world had been an eye-opener, and she knew she had to up her game or be devoured by this colossal organisation. An exemplary student, she had won all the promotions she had sought.

Chief Petty Officer Jane Fraser said to Darkly, "Would you like to use the men's room before we carry on, sir?"

The noise around them reduced to a level where Darkly felt he could hear himself think. He leaned in close enough to smell her perfume—Jo Malone—one of the few he could identify and which he liked very much. He replied that it wasn't necessary, thanks, and followed her into another long corridor. The sheer enormity of the ship was threatening, never mind the three thousand, five hundred personnel it needed to make it all work. It must have been another three hundred yards before Jane Fraser turned off left, opening the door to a room with four personnel who carried arms and were identified as security.

They checked Darkly off their list, and the shorter of the three said, "Please do as you're asked, Mr Knight, and this won't take long, sir."

"Only as it should be," Darkly said with a whiff of sarcasm, which the Americans either didn't understand or ignored. "Could you take your jacket off and place it on the table, please, sir and stand with your legs apart."

Darkly did as he was asked and tried to make eye contact as they felt his clothing from head to toe and then passed a sensor over his entire body. They then gave him a card with his photo on a lanyard, which he hung around his neck. Not one of them would look him in the eye, a bit of very tight security. They then searched his jacket, its lining and pockets, then pulled out his sensor, which could detect electrical impulses and audio frequencies. Standard issue, which would have been very similar to their own devices. They held it up and said, "This is identified and passed as an instrument you may use."

"I'm going to be about fifteen minutes," Darkly said.

"That's fine, but don't be any longer, as the French security comes in next, and their ETA is twenty-five minutes."

"OK, no problem."

Darkly worked his way around the room, using his ECM and looking under each table and every chair. He had started by putting on his glasses and feeling around the table and at the far end of the wardroom, where the Americans were standing. He started to feel along the edge and underneath the table while taking off his glasses and letting the arm fall below the table, out of sight of the neatly twisted the part that went over his ear. It came apart, and he could feel the slight bulge which held the new fluid and squirted the see-through material into a crevice under the surface of the table. Once the new material was released, it would harden in one minute. He reconnected the earpiece to the arm of his glasses and put them on.

The rest of the security check took five minutes. When he had finished, he nodded to the security officers, exited the room, and was met by Chief Petty Officer Fraser again. She took him to his quarters, where he was to remain for the next few hours, when he would be taken to eat and then back to sleep before checking security after the meeting and flying home the following day.

CHAPTER 5

The delegates had all arrived and had time to collect their thoughts about what they were doing here. Why had the meeting been called on such short notice? What were they doing in the middle of the Atlantic Ocean? Why the top secrecy? Who else was present?

They had all been shown to their cabins, offered refreshments, and then collected and taken to the warship's main wardroom. The main wardroom was below decks, it was obviously heavily insulated, as there was not even the hum of the engines of this great engineering achievement. It was one huge ship which behaved like a great city, never sleeping and constantly listening, snooping, monitoring, and rechecking its own strategy as it ploughed the oceans of the world.

The delegates were Brett Caddick, British Prime Minister; Nathan Wilson, Canadian Prime Minister; Hans Cohl German Chancellor; Chloe Latoure, French Prime Minister; Dan Green, Australian Prime Minister; Ava Wang, New Zealand Prime Minister; and Mikhail Ivan Petrov, Russian President.

The three non-English speaking delegates were provided with the latest translation machines and earphones. There were no other people in the room, no security—no translators or secretaries. No cameras, no microphones or recorders. There were pens and large A4 pads and a good supply of water for each position.

United States President Ethan Miller held his hand up to bring the meeting to order.

Ethan Miller came from a rich American family who had groomed him as president from the moment he was born. He had been educated at home from the ages of five to eight, when he was sent to an exclusive private boarding school, Philips Exeter Academy, New Hampshire. He then went to Harvard University in Cambridge to study political science. He excelled at rowing and fencing. He studied at Cambridge University, England, for one year during his course. He rowed in the Boat Race in 1986. Cambridge won. He took it as his win, but then, he would have, as he had been raised this way. He was a six-foot athlete, fair-haired like his mother, although grey had started to show through. He chose for his wife the daughter of one of the richest families in the States. Emily was a patient woman. She bore him three children, whom she'd had to bring up herself as Ethan pursued his all-consuming career in politics. She was just under five feet tall and suffered because of her weight. She was intelligent without being academic. She put up with his numerous affairs and always supported him in all his career endeavours. He had bullied her and didn't listen to much of what she said. His friends were those of his party, as they viewed him with suspicion and had to put up with his sly ways of going about business. However, sweet lady that she was, she ignored his behaviour and lived a remarkably happy and equable life, revolving around the three children and many charities, where she was well-respected.

The room finally fell silent as the powerful leader of the Western world spoke with confidence.

"First of all, thank you all for coming such a long way without knowing what the agenda is about and having the trust in my call for help and being here today."

"We have all seen the extraordinary weather patterns over the last several years. There has been heavier rain than ever recorded in some areas with resulting floods and areas with great drought, much higher heat waves than ever with fires, and crop erosion. We have also seen lower temperatures than ever recorded. At the same time, the ice caps are getting smaller, and sea levels are starting to rise. People are dying in your countries. Tropical rain forests are disappearing at an alarming rate to service our rapacious demands for food. In the USA, we have been recording many special weather patterns over the last twenty years. We have looked at Copernicus in Europe, jet streams, sea temperatures, and patterns of ice erosion, and we currently have 10,000 scientists monitoring every piece of data we can get our hands on. Believe me, we have sweated blood and spent long hours of discussion and 2.3 billion dollars on the figures I'm about to give you."

"These are the conclusions. These figures I'm about to give you go up exponentially. Six months from today's date, the temperature of the earth will start to increase by one degree. The end of month two, which is eight months from today, that temperature will rise by a further two degrees. In month three, the increase will be another four degrees, and human life will be extinguished. We won't be here."

There was silence in the room. For one whole minute, you could have heard a pin drop.

The murmur started as a small whisper. It then raised to a clamour, and in the end, some delegates were shouting questions and demanding answers.

Ethan Miller raised his hand again. The noise level didn't change. He started to talk and eventually shouted. It took him a few minutes to get the level down so he could be heard.

"We have two main problems. One: worldwide overpopulation. Two: pollution from manufacturing and growth. I've got a separate paper from Oxford University England, backing up what I am saying. Read it. It's all there in black and white."

He pointed to the images on the wall of the wardroom, which displayed the areas of the world he was referring to, namely, China, Korea, India, and parts of Africa, Japan, South America, and Indonesia.

"Together, we can solve this problem, but we can only do it together. We all have access to military strength. We divide these areas between us. We attack the nearest or most easily reached populations and areas of large manufacture, and we destroy those areas with our military power.

"We have no time to discuss this, as we need to save the world now, and this is our only chance."

There was complete silence for over a minute, and then a whole cacophony of noise erupted again, as if in a single voice.

"You have to be joking!"

"No, never, not a chance!"

"Is this all true?"

"Atrocious, disgraceful!"

Hans Cohl, the German Chancellor, picked his pad up and threw it violently down on the table, pushing his chair back so it fell and clattered on the floor. He strode towards the door and went to open it. It was locked.

"What the fuck?" he said in a rage.

"You completely mad or what? I'm not staying a minute longer. You're a criminal for keeping us all locked up. What are you up to?"

Brett Caddick sidled towards Ethan Miller as though wanting to talk.

"Button it for now, Brett. Remember, you knew all about this."

The extreme turmoil carried on a further thirty minutes, blanking out Brett Caddick's mild protestations of denial. The delegates had no opportunity to ask, speak, or shout their questions, fears, and speculations. They were ignored in all the noise and confusion.

Ethan Miller stood up and said, "I didn't expect you all to react like this. It's obvious we all need more time. Let me just remind you that China and their disgusting habit of eating wild animal has introduced not only the SARS virus in 2002 but the 2020 Covid-19 crisis.They certainly have not come clean about the circumstances, and it thrust the entire planet into utter chaos, economic downturn, and many deaths. In fact, we will probably never know."

Hans Cohl said, "I need to get back tonight."

Dan Green added, "Me too. I can't wait to get out of this hellhole, mate."

Nathan Wilson said, "I need to return tomorrow morning at the latest."

Brett Caddick said, "Yes, I think we all need to get back. I don't think anything will be agreed upon here."

Chloe la Tourre added, "You Brits are going to side with the

States anyway. It was probably all fixed between you two before our meeting."

Mikhail Petrov said, "Yes, I wondered about that too."

Brett Caddick said, "Not at all. I knew no more than the rest of you before we met today!"

Ethan Miller scanned the room. "OK, OK, OK. I can see you are all upset. It's what I hoped wouldn't happen. The facts, unfortunately, are as I have set them out to you. We really have extraordinarily little time left. I suggest I call you all personally in three days, at which time I can talk to you all one to one. We should meet here again quite soon, as it is essential to work out the finer details. Please do not discuss this with anyone else, or absolute calamity will result. If you can all make your way back to your cabins, your own security will be able to coordinate your departure times. I hope you all have a safe journey home."

CHAPTER 6

In another part of the ship, Simon Knight had wondered how long the meeting would take. There was a knock on his cabin door. He got off the bunk and opened the door.

"Good afternoon, sir. Jane Fraser again, to inform you your PM is going up on deck in about thirty minutes. I'll come back to escort you to his cabin then."

Simon Knightly could tell she liked what she saw by the looks she snuck at him. He smiled at her and said, "Thank you very much, Chief Petty Officer."

"Gee, you Brits are so polite."

They looked at each other and laughed.

"Hey, there's a question I want to ask. May I?"

"Come into the cabin. I don't want you feeling uncomfortably standing in the corridor. You can ask me anything you like."

She came in and let the door click shut.

"Are you OK for time? Are you needed anywhere else?" Darkly asked.

"Not until I take you to Mr Caddick's cabin. Oh, and I've got my radio with me so if they need me, I can just answer it. Now, there is a rumour that you have a nickname and no one knows what it is. Is that right? Something about being in the special forces?"

Simon Knight let out a sudden burst of laughter, feeling as silly as he had the first time he had tried to kiss Katherine Smith in year ten, when he was fourteen on the playing fields at school, overlooking where she lived.

"Well, yes, it's true. I was in the Special Boat Services, and we were seconded to work with special forces sometimes—and we did have nicknames. How the hell did your guys find out?"

"I won't lie to you. Our security did a check on you because I said I thought you looked like a film star and found out about your work— with the Royal Marines and then with the Special Boat Services. Then one of the other guys who had worked with the British Special Forces said you all had nicknames."

He turned to his left, and as he did so, their hands touched. It felt like an electric shock had gone through his arm. He could see her tense up too, and at the same moment, they both moved towards each other. He held her hand and she squeezed his as he put his other hand up to the side of her face, stroking the side of her cheek as they brought their lips together.

Their bodies came together as he stroked Jane's back and she held him around the waist. Their lips touched again, and they enjoyed a long lingering kiss. Their tongues explored each other as they became more comfortable and eased themselves onto the edge of the bed. Darkly held Jane's back, and she groaned and arched towards him. They kicked their shoes off and got more comfortable on the bed. He started to undo the buttons down the front of her tunic and kissed her neck, which made Jane moan at his tender touch. She ran her fingers down his shirt, parting the top buttons and running her fingers through the dark hair on his chest.

Jane was kissing the side of Darkly's neck, flicking her tongue onto his skin as she ran her lips down to his shoulder. Darkly found Jane's ear with his tongue and carefully followed the many contours around the edge, finally letting his tongue push into the middle, making Jane shiver with expectation as they stroked each other's bodies. Darkly had unbuttoned more of Jane's tunic and released the buttons on her blouse so he could slide his hand across to cup her pert breast in his hand. Taking her erect nipple between his fingers he leaned over and allowed his tongue to caress the end and around the radius, which made Jane squeal in pleasure.

Jane undid all the buttons on Darkly's shirt and let her hand slide down. She undid his button and took the zipper down on his trousers, and he lifted his torso for her to remove them and to free his erect manhood. Jane bent down and took it in her mouth, using her tongue and lips to make Darkly gasp with delight. He now wanted to give her the same pleasure, so they both took off the rest of Jane's clothes for Darkly to slide his tongue up and down Janes wet vulva, slowly letting her get the full satisfaction of that sensation until he found her clitoris, which he sucked and licked to make Jane's hips pulse with the movement of his tongue.

Jane put her hand down to Darkly's face and pulled him up until their lips found each other again. She settled him between her opened legs, which allowed Jane to help him into her pulsating body. They both looked down to enjoy that moment and began to move together as though they had known each other for a long time. Darkly used his hips to achieve the deepest possible penetration, and Jane used beautiful pelvic movements to make the most of his stiff penis. They enjoyed the mounting joy of being together and managed to reach their crescendo at the same moment, heaving and grinding into one another while trying not to shriek out in happiness, urgency, and sheer joy. Neither of them had ever reached this plateau of exploding eroticism before, which made their bodies shudder from the extreme arousal.

As Jane lay back trying to catch her breath, Darkly said, "I wasn't expecting that." He was panting and gently caressing Jane's beautiful curves, smiling into her eyes.

"Nor was I, but, oh boy, was that something else."

They both laughed. Jane rolled onto the top of Darkly's body and positioned her head so their lips locked together. Jane pulled her head away and said, "Hey, we'd better get moving, or we'll be in trouble."

Jane went into the bathroom with her clothes, and Darkly got dressed. When she came out, Darkly quickly went into the bathroom. When he came out, she was all neat and tidy in her chief petty officer's uniform.

"Ready for escort duty, sir."

Darkly said, "Yes, I've heard about you navy types."

Jane said, "Well, I've heard a bit about you special forces types, but I never thought I would meet one who made me feel like you did!"

Darkly opened the door for her, and they went out into the corridor, headed for the wardroom. When they got to the corridor which led down to the door into the wardroom, security stopped Jane and checked Darkly's tag and photo, then motioned for him to go in alone. As he entered the room, there were only three technicians working on the overhead equipment. They paid him no attention and could easily identify the table where he had planted the listening device, as the furniture had barely been moved. He felt underneath the table and easily got his index fingernail under one end, lifting and peeling the solidified cylindrical tube away from the crevice where it had lain hidden and curling it into his palm. He dropped it into his trouser pocket. He got a small pad out of the same pocket and opened it up, drew the pencil out of the sheath on its side, and wrote eleven numbers on a page he had flicked open. Besides that, he wrote the letter D. Back in the corridor, he rejoined Jane, who informed him that his plane was ready for the PM's flight and they could go to his cabin straight away. They could collect his things later.

Outside the PM's cabin, he knocked. Brett Caddick came to the door quickly. He looked extremely pale, which Darkly mentioned.

Brett Caddick said, "I don't think you would believe me if I told you, which I can't, incidentally, because everything is strictly confidential, as you know."

The three of them made their way up towards the deck, and Darkly carried the PM's briefcase to a plane similar to the one he had flown in. Brett took the case off Darkly, climbed up the ladder onto the wing, and hoisted himself into the front cockpit. Darkly nodded to Brett, who wished him a safe journey.

"Thanks, Darkly. I feel very safe in your hands," he shouted, although it was all lost in the din going on around them. He gave him a wink, and the canopy closed as he was putting on his helmet. Darkly nodded and thought Brett Caddick looked a lonely and small figure, uneasy and struggling with what was going on. Darkly turned and strode across the deck and stood beside Jane as the Pratt and

Whitney engine of the F-35B Lightning II roared into a new higher pitch. Having received the OK from the ground crew, it started its vertical take-off, reaching 200 feet before it started tipping forward slightly as it quickly gained speed, climbing higher into the clear blue sky and away.

As they walked briskly back to Darkly's cabin, Jane said, "You never did tell me your nickname."

Reaching his cabin, they entered, and Darkly took the piece of paper from his pocket. He took her by the waist and held her tenderly. "It's Darkly, and here's my mobile number."

Jane burst out laughing and punched him in the chest.

"You goon. Hey, but you're a cool dude, and I would like, somehow, to keep in touch."

Without hesitation, Darkly said, "Me too. What happened was amazing, and I can honestly say I'm not in the habit of seducing young ladies like this. Yes, I would like to make a stab at keeping in touch."

"Well, Darkly," Jane started giggling and was only just able to say, "I'm not sure what you just said, but I like the gist of it. I wrote my mobile number here just in case!" She handed him a sheet of perfumed paper with flowers on it. "Come on. I better get you up on deck quickly."

They made their way up onto the upper deck.

"Sir, your flight is ready—if you would like to climb aboard," the flight manager said as he motioned towards the fighter's RAF insignia.

Darkly thanked him and turned to Jane, shaking her hand.

He climbed the ladder, stepped onto the wing and into the cockpit, and placed his bag beside the side of the seat. He strapped himself in, slipped the canopy to the closed position, and put on his helmet.

"Good afternoon, Sergeant Knight. It's Gary Goodman here on the controls. Hold on tight. We've already got clearance for takeoff, and I'll have you back in Blighty within the hour."

The guy with the bats gave the all-clear, and Gary gave it full thrust. The noise was incredible. The seat thumped him in the back. A *whoosh*, and they were over the end of the ships' flight deck and airborne. He had never experienced anything like that before. Absolutely a boy's dream. He loved this side of his job—most of the time, anyway.

CHAPTER 7

Darkly's father, Colin, was quick-witted and had a blond head of hair that caught the eye, along with his height. He had worked at the post office, where he had pounded the streets of South London, delivering letters for years. It was during this time that he became a vocal member of the Communication Workers Union. He avidly attended all their meetings, often giving his own view, which increasingly argued for workers' rights.

He had put in for a promotion but was told his union connection would make it difficult to progress within the post office. He felt overlooked and undervalued and would always drop into the pub near work for a drink after the union meetings with his workmates.

He was a good all-around sportsman and excelled at tennis, which he played for his works team. He was tall and had maintained a muscular frame. This gave him a distinct advantage when serving, and his reach made him a popular player. Although he played to a high standard, he slowly became disillusioned with the competition, which did not stretch his ability. He would drop in for a few pints after tennis. He had looked at a local tennis club where the competition would have been higher, but he could not afford the fees. So, he got into the habit of taking a small flask of whiskey into work, which, he argued, made the afternoons go by quicker.

Darkly's mother, Muriel, was a sweet-tempered, patient person who loved her job working in the kitchen at their local primary school. She loved the contact with the children and had not had the exam success of her sister, Brenda, who had got into teacher training college, passed all her exams, and worked at the local secondary school, teaching English.

Auntie Brenda had been able to buy a house in Worcester Park, whereas when Muriel had married Colin Knight; they lived in a council flat in South Morton. Muriel had excelled in Domestic Science at school and had worked at night school to gain the exams required to work in the kitchens, providing meals at lunchtime.

Colin's drinking grew worse. He smelt of alcohol at work, which led to numerous warnings. Following the third written warning, he was fired for being unfit for duty. It was a serious situation, and the union could not help him or defend the position he had created for himself.

Life had been bearable while Colin had a permanent job, although there had not been any money left over at the end of the month. Colin had looked at the Open University after it opened in 1969 and followed its televised programs. He had hoped a promotion at the post office would allow them to afford the fees.

Darkly had been born in 1978 and remained an only child even though Colin and Muriel would have liked another one. Now that there were three mouths to feed and the rent to pay, there wasn't enough to pay for the fees for OU. Muriel did more than her contract required, as she arranged the menus, ordered the food, and cooked, but there was no possibility to earn more than a part-time wage.

Darkly was about two years old when Colin had started to drop into their local pub on his way home from the post office, in addition to the sessions after the union meetings and the tennis nights. Darkly was six when he could recall he had his own tea with his mother. She would then prepare a meal for her and Colin. He remembered coming downstairs occasionally to find his mother eating without his father, whose tea had been dutifully left for him on the table, where it had grown cold. He would be woken up by his father raising his voice to Muriel, and they would have bitter arguments. Occasionally, Colin would throw the plate onto the table, cascading it all over the side and onto the floor. He would then push Muriel out of his way as he aimed for the front room and the whisky bottle. None of this made much sense to the young boy, except that he would hear his mother cry out in pain after scuffling and slapping noises.

Darkly remembered being put to bed either by his mother or her sister, who used to come round to keep these warring parents calm while she took him upstairs and read him a story.

No one could have expected what happened next in Darkly's eighth year. He returned home from school, opened the front door, saw the blue and red marks from the rope around his lovely mothers' neck, which he remembered to this day. The overturned stool lay beneath her. There were nail scratches on the wallpaper beside her still body. It hung down from a spindle on the landing above her. He could see beyond this horrendous sight into the kitchen. The table had been laid for his tea, and her shopping bag was on the table chair, where she always put it when she came back from the shops.

He started crying because his mother was a peculiar shade of grey, and she was quite still. He didn't want her like this. He sank to his knees and hung onto the hem of her pleated skirt. Mrs Jenkins, their neighbour, came running through the door, alerted by the sound of his gulping cries of grief. She lived in the house next door and wanted to see if she could help. It was too late.

The next three weeks were a complete blur. He didn't recall anything until he walked into his auntie's house, which was to become his new home.

CHAPTER 8

Darkly rode his bike back to Number 10. The PM wasn't in, so he went straight up to his office. It wasn't the smallest office he had ever seen, but you could not have swung a cat round. He smiled in amusement at the reference because it had nothing to do with housecats. It referred to the barbaric British Services punishment of flogging with the cat-o'-nine-tails. He had to check the security shifts and all the comings and goings—who had visited and who had been on duty and their comments, nothing unusual. He signed them off on his computer and picked up his mobile and phoned Matt Drayson.

"What do you want to do with the X15?"

"Best come over here, as the decipher equipment is here in my office. Say about 4 p.m.?"

"Yes, that's fine for me. See you then."

He had the time to attend other duties at Number 10 before he went over to MI5. As he was going downstairs, he saw Brett Caddick. He had never seen him look so stressed, fretful, and agitated, and he wondered just what had gone off in that wardroom on the USS *George Bush*. He cycled the short distance to MI5 HQ, parked his bike securely, and made his way in. Matt picked him up from reception and took him up to his office.

"Oh, hi, Simon. Have you got our little trial with you?"

Darkly took the case out of his pocket, opened it, took the length of sillicon out, and laid it on the desk.

"OK, let's get it onto the cipher machine. It will take a few minutes, and then we download the decipher onto the computer. Then we can listen in and see if it's any good."

Darkly laid the tube-shaped piece of clear silica on the receiver of the deciphering machine. Matt Drayson closed the lid and set the machine in motion.

"It should take about five minutes to withdraw the information, and then we'll transfer that signal onto the computer, which will let us listen to the transcript which has been programmed onto this computer. Some of the other trials have failed, but there have been successes, so this has the potential to be extremely useful if it works. Thanks for setting the trial up on short notice. Where did you plant it?"

"In the end, I didn't have much choice. I used a meeting the PM was having yesterday, which should be interesting, although you may be able to tell who was there from the vocabulary. I was able to introduce it between joints underneath a table in the main meeting room. The whole room was scanned several times, and X15 was not detected. It was as easy to introduce as it was to extricate. It must have set quickly, and I could not detect any smell which could have given away its position."

There was a ping from the computer programme.

"OK, I think she's ready. I need to key in the code, and we'll have a listen."

Matt pressed a few keys, and the recording burst into life. The beginning was garbled, and there was some interference initially, but it settled down; it must have picked up all the dialogue, as there were no gaps.

After fifteen minutes, Matt and Darkly looked at each other. They had sat in complete silence, sometimes looking at the other, sometimes at the floor. They were speechless. They could not believe what they had just heard.

Matt said, "Shall we have a short break and reflect a little?"

Darkly said, "Good idea. I need a pee, anyhow."

He left the office and headed for the men's room, where he was immediately able to assess the ramifications for him personally. He should not have had access to this top-secret intel. Added to this, he had inadvertently allowed MI5 into the circle of knowledge, which meant they could not ignore his position. It placed him in an extremely dangerous situation. They would definitely consider his total elimination, which would prevent him from leaking anything he knew. His next moves would have to be carefully anticipated, using well-thought-out tactics. The shit had hit the fan, and he hadn't seen it coming.

They took their places around the computer amplifiers as though they had not heard correctly, and the rest of the recording would change. In silence, Matt restarted the computer. It went on for a further twenty-five minutes. The recording did not pick up the final ten minutes of the meeting, but really, they didn't need to hear any more. Again, they sat for two whole minutes after it had finished. They were both breathless and couldn't believe what they had heard. It hadn't got any better as it progressed. They had originally decided to make notes about performance, clarity, and any indistinct noises, but they had both stopped taking notes as the seriousness of the content revealed itself.

Matt said, "It did have some fading, and certainly, you could hear chair movement."

Darkly said, "Chairs and farts too."

They both laughed, looked embarrassed that they had laughed, and looked at their hands.

Matt was the first to speak. "That made the hair on the back of my neck stand on end."

Darkly said, "I've got sweat running down my back. What the fuck do we do with this info?"

Matt said, "Just what I was thinking."

Darkly said, "From where I'm sitting, it's international espionage. It's very serious, and I could go to jail for this, even if it was unintentional and at the request of MI5."

Matt said, "Yes, I get your point." Darkly sensed a lack of conviction in this statement. In fact, he was already getting the unnerving feeling that he could not trust Matt at all. He detected more of a *How can I save my own hide and come out of this best?* from the man's behaviour. It wasn't like dealing with your own kind, who would give their life for you and often had.

Darkly said, "I think this is too much to take in and that we should finish our meeting now and arrange another time, when we have had time to work out what each of us has to do next."

Matt said, "Good idea. Give me a ring tomorrow."

Darkly said, "OK, Matt, I'll do that. Until I speak to you tomorrow."

Darkly could not wait to get out of there and down the stairs and into the street, where he took in a deep breath and smelt the good old Thames. Deep down, he thought only of all the innocent lives this would waste. The white cloud of death and destruction. The white cloud represented darkness, shadows, and death. It mad made him shiver.

At the same moment that Darkly jumped on his bike and headed back to Number 10, Matt had sprinted up three flight of stairs to knock on the door of Colin Murray (HUMINT), head of the overt overseas collection and analysis of human intelligence in support of the UK's national security.

Matt knocked on the door and entered. "Hi, Uncle. I've got something interesting for you."

Darkly had been back at work and finished his shift when he finally got home. He sat down in his favourite armchair. He sank his head in his hands. He had never been in such a position ever before, and this was not of his own doing. He could just see the headlines.

"Head of Number Ten Security Involved in International Espionage."

That would look good on his CV. Then he thought that if all he and Matt had listened to was true, his CV didn't really matter. One way or another, real lives were at stake. He was sure Matt would discuss all the intel with his superiors and therefore could not be trusted. In his estimation, M15 was a real can of worms—and not to be trusted.

CHAPTER 9

Darkly had decided to have counselling as he came off active service in the Royal Navy. He had seen too many of his old mates leave active service and become unable to cope with Civvy Street. Any government, he thought, fell short when it came to dealing with the mental issues active servicemen and women go through during the transition from using a gun to protect oneself to landing on the street with a pocketful of money, no job. He had seen many of his friends fall into the black pit. Service personnel are given little guidance about money and finances when they leave active duty. He had seen fewer than 20 per cent turn out successful.

Darkly had two things in his favour: (1) he could afford the counselling and was making good progress, and (2) he had Auntie Brenda. Auntie B had advised him to put his money in bricks and mortar—hence, his early decision to buy the house in Pimlico. The area had been run-down, with prostitution and drugs on the street in the open when he and Auntie B had first looked at it. It was such a bad area then, and the house was in such poor condition, but it was one of the few houses he could afford. The mortgage was small, and over the years, he had paid it off.

His counselling from the NHS had lasted for six sessions. This was not enough for Darkly. He needed more therapy, and he would have to go privately. The initial six sessions had been useful, but the dark thoughts remained. However, he was able to afford to pay for as many sessions as he needed with a private counsellor.

He had really got on with his NHS counsellor and was at first reluctant to consider a move. In the end, he had no other choice. His new counsellor, Julia Wheeton, made it easier to arrange the sessions to fit in with his busy work schedule, and it seemed she would be there for him for the long haul. She was small and slim, with dark hair which came down past her shoulders. Her clothing was smart and comfortable. She quickly put the idea to Darkly that he could paint in his spare time and articulate his feelings through his artwork. She would give him subjects to cover, and he would have to bring the painting to their next meeting. At the end of the first session, she asked him to let the painting describe how he felt during that day. He was extremely surprised by the images he painted.

His first figure was a man standing with his head in a black cloud. The image disturbed him, and it had taken two sessions to discuss it fully. The next painting involved a human in the fetal position within a human head, using mostly shades of black with the occasional splash of red. As therapy progressed, more frightening images came out; there was one where Darkly had painted a figure crouched in a corner with one hand covering his face and the other hand on top of his head. At first, he thought his dark moods were becoming worse.

Eighteen months later, Julia said he had been to enough therapy meetings, and if he ever felt he needed her help again, he could return. Considering all the unfortunate service people who lacked this process that benefitted Darkly so much, he felt blessed and humble.

CHAPTER 10

Three hours later, he had some rough ideas going through his head. He realised MI5 would come after him one way or another and he needed to be as prepared as possible. It could be life-threatening or, at the very least, life-changing. So he needed to put together a plan and be in front of whatever they decided to do next.

Would the US president's military strikes be considered criminal warfare? It would also make the US the most dominant manufacturing country globally, and had Ethan Miller put all this together to achieve that end. Would all the nations in the North Atlantic meeting pull together? He was sure they eventually would.

Darkly's time in the Royal Marines had taught him that two heads are better than one at sorting out a problem. He had fallen into a no-win situation, one he had not chosen but which the powers of MI5 could not ignore.

He cecided to visit his oldest friend from university and so it was that he found himself knocking on the study door of Professor Paul English DBE FRS Master, his old roommate at Cambridge University, who had gone on to get a first in computer sciences and decided to pursue an academic life. Some years later, he was now master of the faculty. They had kept in touch over the years. Darkly was godfather to Paul and Jenny's first child, Hazel. He stood about a foot lower than Darkly. He had kept his slim figure and all his blond thatch. This kept Darkly in touch for birthdays and Christmas and

Easter and countless other times throughout the year when Darkly was free.

"How are you? Still in one piece, Simon? I'm glad you phoned. It got me out of a stuffy and boring dinner at Churchill, getting too long in the tooth for all that stuff. Hope you're staying the evening, as Judith's expecting you for supper?"

"Yes, please, I don't want to miss any of Jenny's cooking."

"When you phoned, it sounded serious, so I thought we would be better here where it's quiet and no kids. We can nip home later if that's OK, mate."

"Yeah, that sounds great. Thanks, Paul. Yes, I've got myself in a bit of a fix."

The prof ushered Darkly towards one of two comfortable-looking and well-used armchairs. Darkly gladly sank into its springy horsehair leather luxury.

"We lost the coal fires when we moved into this new building life is always the same: three steps forward and two back." They both laughed, and Paul poured himself a beer, giving Darkly a lime and soda.

Darkly took his time going through the impossible situation into which he had stumbled. Once Paul English understood the whole picture and Darkly's impossible position, they discussed the abuse to humanity suggested by the US president—the world dominance in both politics and manufacturing and the American future military strength. Politically, would the perpetrators of this crime survive the expected public outcry?

Darkly predicted MI5 would soon be paying him a lot of aggressive attention.

"Can we be sure the estimated temperature rise hasn't been egged up and that the climate change figures are completely accurate?"

"I've been on the sites the president mentioned, and they are all bona fide and still providing scientific evidence."

"If that's the case, we must take them at face value. This gives us little space to work with. What can I do, Simon, to help your predicament? Was there anything you had in mind?"

"Yes. I have thought of nothing else since I heard the tape. I've been going over and over what I heard, and as much as I would like it to be different, we are where we are."

"Correction, Simon, old friend: you are where you are." Paul started laughing, and although coming to it later, Simon got the joke and started laughing too.

"Sorry, Paul. My mind has been so taken up with this, I'm having difficulty seeing any way through. However, there may be something. But to be honest, the reason I'm here is to have a second thought on it with someone I can trust. It's impossible to trust anyone else. What did occur to me was about a way to stop the military computers."

"Well, computers are my business. What you're asking has never been done before."

"First things first, Simon: we need total security."

"Whatsapp?"

"Only communication we can use, chum. I think I've got all I need from you. Funnily enough, I gave my master's students, which was their fourth year, a similar project recently. I might be able to do some of their work. If using a computer virus to stop world share trading would be marked out of ten, three of them attained level 7 or 8. OK if we head home and make tea with the chimps?"

"Perfect with me Paul—and thanks."

"I've agreed to nothing yet, mate."

This last comment could have sent Darkly a negative message—that he had not known the Paul of old would make until his faithful friend had considered all aspects a decision before agreeing to anything.

As Paul unlocked the front door of his four-bedroom semi-detached house on Trumpington Road in the suburbs of Cambridge, he announced, "We're home." The whole family emerged to cluster round Darkly, kissing him, hugging him, and generally clamouring to get their part of him, pulling him to come and read to them or see their latest creation. The children were Hazel, fifteen; his goddaughter, Max, thirteen and sporty; and Ned, eleven, who made up for his small stature with his arty personality. Darkly finally made it through to the kitchen, where Jenny was putting the final touches on a lasagna she had just taken out of the oven. She flung her arms around him and kissed him, followed by a big hug.

"Simon, lovely to see you. You look as fit as ever—and twice as gorgeous. Any lucky lady we need to meet yet?"

"Mummy loves Simon," chanted Max.

"Yes, I do," replied Jenny.

"Daddy loves Simon too, you know."

By this time, everyone was trying to speak at once and laughing.

Darkly had turned slightly red and looked at Paul for support, who looked back at his old friend and shrugged his shoulders.

"Tea's ready. Sit down, everybody. Hazel and Ned can sit next to Simon," Jenny shouted above the din. She turned round and went through the wide alcove into the kitchen. The dining room had been knocked through into the lounge so all three rooms were interconnected. Plates were passed around, and everyone helped themselves to the lettuce, tomatoes, and cucumbers.

"I grew the lettuce, Simon. Look, it's all down the side of the garden," said Hazel.

"I grew the cucumber in the greenhouse," Ned shouted.

"Jenny's tomatoes … I don't know how she finds the time. They taste so fantastic compared to the shop-bought ones," Paul said.

"I laid the table, good, eh?" Max said.

"No more bragging, please. Everyone, let poor Simon have his tea in peace," said Jenny, winking at Darkly."

The quiet lasted for seven seconds.

"Have you spoken to the prime minister this week? Did you go to Buckingham Palace like you said during the last visit? Have you seen anybody famous today? Wait until I tell them at school tomorrow you've been for tea."

Darkly bade his farewells to his adopted family and cycled back to the station in time to catch the 9:39 back to St Pancras, arriving at 10:32. He had brought his bike to Cambridge, knowing Paul only went around on his bike, which meant they could both cycle back together to his house for tea.

CHAPTER 11

Darkly had cycled the four miles to his house in Pimlico and mounted the curb on the dual-suspension mountain bike, his vehicle of choice for London traffic. He wheeled along the alley beside his garden, rising out of his seat so that he could see any movement or uninvited guests, in the house or garden. In his current position, he could be a target for MI5.

Think ahead, and no surprises.

He stopped beside what appeared to be a solid section of fencing. Sliding a small piece of wood to one side, he flicked a catch, and a narrow door granted him passage inside to his garden. He bounded up the steps to the back door of the house, checked the piece of chest hair (as the hair on his head was too short), was in place from two days ago and entered, and parked his bike. He had decided he never wanted alcohol to take over his life like it had with his father

Over the years he had learnt to forgive the poor man, for his weakness. However from that day on, the image of his mother hanging in the stairwell of their home was etched in mind. He poured himself a lime and bitter lemon from the fridge, took it to the front room. In the dark, he relaxed into his leather armchair, took a good draught from the pint glass, and thought over the previous forty-eight hours.

He had bought the house nearly twenty years earlier with the money he had saved from his overseas postings. When he had walked down the street with Auntie B to meet the estate agent to view, he had been asked whether he was "in the business". He had been very young then and a bit wet behind the ears and hadn't connected the paper taped across most of the windows; the girls waiting along the pavement and by the gates and the men hanging back skulking in the shadows; the peeling paint on the doors and windows; and the discarded bedding and furniture littered around where there should have been flowers. It took him a second or two to comprehend what "in the business" meant, and he looked at Auntie B, blushing a crimson red to match the sky at either end of darkness. Later, alone again, they both nearly ended up on the floor with laughter when Auntie B said, "What the hell did he think I was to make a comment like that?"

The slick young salesman, obviously studying the part for Uriah Heap in a Charles Dickens novel, had realised he was a genuine buyer when Darkly had answered, "I'm in the Royal Marines."

He and Auntie B had chosen the house because it was "run-down and in need of immediate building attention", and it was all he could afford. The salesman then said, "Well, sir, madam, your hard-earned money is always best placed in bricks and mortar." As this was what Auntie B had advised him in the first place, after hearing this piece of advice, they couldn't look at each other for fear of corpsing again.

"He didn't even rub his hands together when he said it."

When they had brought themselves under control again, they discussed the house.

"It's in a rough state, Simon."

"The lads always have people they know who can just about get anything done, Auntie B, and they all know plumbers, joiners, sparkies, and the like. That is not a problem, and they would be trusted to do the work for me. My biggest worry is the cost of it all."

"Well, it doesn't all have to be done at once. For example, you could just about put up with the kitchen. A good clean and a can of paint covers a multitude of sins. You always said when you joined the army, 'If it moves, salute it. If it doesn't, paint it.'"

Darkly laughed and said, "You're right."

"You could apply for a grant for a new boiler and central heating from the council, save you some money. Rip all the carpets out. Put a new one in the bedroom after you've had it painted. I'll sort the curtains and duvets and linens and towels as a housewarming present from me and Sadie. She's been saving her pocket money, you know." She smiled warmly at him.

"And you can take the bed in your room, which is quite new, anyway."

"You are a marvel. Thanks ever so much." He gave her a great hug.

"If you need to borrow a little for the carpets, that's OK, too."

The house was bought, and slowly, work had began.

While Darkly sat in his armchair, and focused on his present predicament. He spent some time working through what he knew and what he could anticipate, also in the equasion the things he did not know. He was confident that bringing Paul England on board was a good step and also one he had to protect. First, this was the highest level of intel and had to be handled very carefully. One false move, and the ceiling came down. MI5 could either trust Darkly or, if they didn't, quickly terminate him. The first step, however, would be to fire a warning shot across his bow. If they didn't trust him, with whom might he share his info? Who would they expect him to tell, or would they think he might go public? If they could trust him, would he behave like an obedient civil servant? Would he remain quiet? If so, could they use him again? That was an interesting thought. They would have to bug his house, anyway; that fact was certain. How should Darkly react? They would be sure he would think this all out for himself. So, he needed to tell them what they wanted to hear and let them know he would expect a lot of shit.

CHAPTER 12

Darkly received a telephone call from Matthew at MI5 the following morning to meet him at eleven in a café in central London; things were running to plan and as he had expected.

The Kensington Café Bar was the venue. Darkly knew its position and entered off the street and walked along the long line of tables opposite the bar and food area to the end table where Matt put his hand up in recognition. Special service operatives were taught to assess everyone they dealt with. What was their breathing like? Were they sweating? Eye contact? If they couldn't look you in the eye, something was wrong, and Matt's eye contact was not happening. He knew what to expect. Matt said, "Can I get you a coffee, Simon?"

Darkly said, "Expresso—black, please."

As Matt left the seat opposite him, two suited men peeled off from the queue at the counter, and one sat next to Darkly and the other opposite him. Matt returned and sat next to the man opposite. Darkly was hemmed in apart from jumping up onto the table; he had no choice but to stay where he was. The man sitting opposite him was in his fifties and had clearly never seen active service. He wore spectacles and looked like an exceedingly nasty piece of work. He had a lean face, greying hair, no scars, and a well-groomed appearance. Darkly knew he could have got hold of his throat with one hand, lifted him out of his seat, head-butted him, raised himself up, and used his right elbow to destroy the nose of the guy to his right. He could strike Matt in the throat and make his escape, but something

46

told him to stay put and find out what they had to say—as if he didn't know.

The guy with the glasses spoke in a soft, menacing voice, authoritatively calm and modulated. Darkly thought he came over as creepy, mean and confident, superior even.

"Listen to what I'm about to say: don't move, don't speak. You are in a very precarious position and could be in grave danger. We know your movements, where you live, where you go to the gym. You need to do exactly what I tell you, or we will take you out. Do you understand so far?"

Darkly nodded.

"Good. You are to forget what you heard on the tape. You are to speak to no one about any part of this. You are to go about your duties as if nothing has happened. Is that understood?"

Darkly nodded again.

"You are not to contact Matt again unless he contacts you. Have I made myself completely clear? You do understand?"

Darkly said, "Yes, I do."

"Finish your coffee, and don't follow us. Good day to you."

The door to the café had been opened, and the three of them went out onto the street and got onto a waiting car which then sped off.

Darkly sat for a while, quietly thinking. During the meeting, he had been planning who to take out first and with which and most efficient blow, and who next, as he would leave the least able until last—whether to kill them where they sat or leave them alive, which would give himself more time to escape. They were bound to have accomplices watching the proceedings, so his escape was as important as his physical elimination inside the café. However, that had not been necessary. OK, round one to them. Get back to Number 10.

Darkly walked into Number 10 through the back entrance and immediately made for his own office to think through his strategy.

CHAPTER 13

The evening sun shone across the wood-panelled office of China's President, Chi Mou Yung. Everywhere was quiet, which was just how he liked it at this time of day.

The black phone on his huge, highly polished wooden desk rang in a shrill tone.

"Hello?"

"Hi, Chi Mou. It's Mikhail Petrov. Here we can have a private talk. I have some information I need to discuss with you."

Chi Mou Yung was not used to Mikhail phoning him. He realised it must be of great importance as he had asked for a private talk, which he had never asked for before.

"I understand. This line is completely secure. Mikhail, please go ahead."

"Thank you, Chi Mou. Listen carefully. I was asked to a meeting of all the Western powers who had access to military power. The Americans called the meeting. Their scientists are saying that world pollution has got out of control and the earth's temperature is going to rise within six months, and there is not any way to stop it unless we stop manufacturing. The only way forward is to target all the *non-Western* areas of the world who manufacture and have over population which pollutes the atmosphere, and eradicate these areas using military power." This last part of the call was shouted down the telephone.

The Chinese president had beads of sweat running down the sides of his head, dripping to the ends of his hair and onto his temples. His face was red, and his hands were shaking and so wet he could hardly hold the telephone. He was glad Mikhail was not sitting opposite him and could not see how badly he was reacting to the distressing news.

He was a man who liked to control every move that was made. This new information came as a shock. China controlled over 40 per cent of the world's manufacturing. China's container ships were the largest vessels on the sea. This he liked. This he could control. Stage two of his strategy was to move into his neighbours' territories one by one, which he had already tested out when taking control of Tibet. The West had meekly sat back, and like cowards, they had allowed him to do what he liked. They had even publicly executed innocent people on the streets. The West had sat on their hands, showing they had no stomach for a fight. He planned to constrict any other nation having control, including Russia, who could be useful only in the early stages. Eventually, the Chinese Empire would rule the world. This news of which Mikhail spoke could not be in the plan. It threw him badly.

"Let me think, Mikhail. This is disturbing news. We need to react. I will phone you in forty-eight hours. Goodbye."

CHAPTER 14

Brett Caddick, the British prime minister, sat at his working desk, and his phone rang.

"Hello, Brett Caddick here."

"Hello, sir. Colonel Grant here, GCHQ. We met last December. You may remember there was snow on the ground when you visited."

"Yes, your son's in the Marines, is that right?"

"Spot on, sir. You've got it. I am phoning with some disturbing info you should hear before the Americans. It's from our own satellite. We have picked up Soviet and Chinese mobile nuclear launch pad movements, which could ultimately place many of our Western cities at risk. They have done this before—last June, to be precise. They co-operated on a similar exercise when you used political persuasion to stop their efforts."

"Correct, so they have started a similar exercise?"

"Yes, sir. We have no further information at this time, but the moment anything changes, I'll let you know."

"OK, Colonel Grant. Thanks very much."

Brett Caddick leaned back in his high-backed red leather swivel chair.

So, he thought, *the Russians have brought the Chinese into the ring. I hope it's the last time we trust them with any sensitive information.*

He dialled the US President's direct line.

"What time do call this Brett. it's the middle of the night here."

Brett Caddick ignored Ethan Miller's bullying tone and relayed the information to him.

"Shit's really hit the fan this time Brett. OK, thanks for the call. I'll deal with it on this end. We will keep our eye on this situation. It certainly changes things. Brett, the cat's out of the bag now. Speak later."

Brett Caddick felt violently sick. This had brought the whole scheme forward. They needed to act and change their plans, and he needed to keep on top of the information coming out of GCHQ. If the info was correct, they would have to bring forward their date. He decided now was the time to bring all the chiefs of staff on board and be ready to enlarge the already awful situation outlined by the American president and react with a more serious threat. This would have to take precedence over everything else. He really felt what he was taking part in was very wrong. What else could he do? Let the world burn up in front of their eyes. Who could he ask for help or advice? There was no one, and he was left completely on his own. Completely alone, a potential killer of innocent people.

The red phone rang. It made him jump.

"Yes, Ethan?"

"We need another Atlantic meeting."

"When were you thinking?

"How about yesterday?"

"Ha, ha. Very good, Ethan."

"For fuck's sake, Brett. Tomorrow, same times and coordinates. Do you understand me? This is an emergency." Ethan Miller slammed down the phone.

Brett Caddick phoned Darkly and told him there was another North Atlantic meeting and he would be picked up at 0600 the following morning.

CHAPTER 15

Darkly's phone rang. He looked at the sender.

"Yes, Matt?"

"There's another meeting tomorrow."

"Where the hell do you get your intel?"

"Never mind that; we order you to follow our instructions, and I will deliver another set of spectacles to your office for you to activate the trial using X15."

"To perform an act of espionage against my own government, you mean?"

"May I remind you of the delicate position you have already got yourself into. I am not going to argue with you, Knight. I'll be at your office in half an hour." The phone went dead.

Darkly whistled and said out loud. "You bastards."

CHAPTER 16

North Atlantic

Darkly could not get used to travelling at 800 mph, 300 feet above the waves. They made the journey in daylight and made sure no other vessels had visual contact with them sweeping left and right in big arcs, which was even more amazing as he looked over his shoulder straight down at the waves. All too soon, the USS *George W Bush* came into sight, and they were hovering over the deck. It still sent a thrill up his spine as the 35-B Lightning 11 fighter started its slow descent onto the lightly rolling deck of the vast aircraft carrier. During his time with the Royal Marines, he had dropped into clearings in the jungle, into compounds in Afghanistan, and onto the tops of buildings. He had been transferred onto submarines at sea. He had landed on hostile beaches from inflatables, sometimes taking enemy fire, but nothing quite beat this. The technical brilliance of the equipment was jaw-dropping, and yet, here he was—all in a day's work. A bump, and they were down.

He followed instructions onto the unsteady deck. As the wind forced him to lean into it, the smell of the aircraft fuel touched his senses, and as he looked up, he made out the smiling face of Chief Petty Officer Jane Foster, her hair taken up into a bun.

They arrived down at the cabin allocated to Sgt Simon Knight. Jane used the plastic card to open the door, and they both entered. Once the door clicked shut, Jane turned towards Darkly and took his face in both of her hands and kissed him on the lips. She then pressed her lips against his temple and let them slip down his cheek to his ear, which she gently tickled with her tongue. Darkly let out a soft murmur and ran his hands down her spine and onto her beautifully defined buttocks. Jane involuntarily wiggled and trembled at his soft, confident touch. She unzipped her skirt, which she let slide down to her feet and kicked it to one side. Darkly undid her tunic and blouse, and Jane undid his shirt and trouser buttons and slowly opened his zip to let them fall to the floor. Darkly looked down at Jane's matching black suspenders and stockings and noticed she was not wearing any other underclothes. He became as hard as a stone. Jane stretched up and clasped her hands around Darkly's neck, pulling herself up as she placed her feet on either side of him on the cabin door and was able to guide him into her very wet vagina. Jane pulled herself up and slowly settled herself down his entire length while Darkly used his hips to create an exotic movement that allowed them a rhythm of extreme pleasure.

They each had to *shush* each other from making too much noise, which might be heard outside the cabin. Darkly slid his hands along Jane's beautiful thighs enough to support her body weight and moved forward to lift her off the door, carefully turn and tenderly place her under him on the small bed. He moved his arms to hold up her legs as he slowly gained more penetration which made Jane moan as she looked up onto Darkly's handsome face and couldn't help herself coming with a massive convulsion of her whole body.

Jane said. "That was amazing, but you didn't come Darkly?"

"Jane, it was enough for me to see you enjoy the moment. I got more than enough from watching you and being part of that—honestly."

"You absolutely sure, Darkly?"

"Really." He gave her a long, lingering kiss as he held her face in his strong hands. He enveloped her in a body hug as they held each other tight and came down from cloud nine and back to some sense of normality.

They had to get moving and tidied themselves up, and checked each other's appearance. They went out onto the corridor, and Jane took control and led him along corridors, up steps, through doors and finally to the Wardroom.

CHAPTER 17

Darkly's next meeting with Matt Drayson was in Regents Park Allotment Garden, located between the corner of Chester Road and the inner circle of the Park. First available bench on the right. He thought it was bizarre the lengths MI5 went to for secrecy. He arrived early and parked his bike behind the bench, just in case he had to make a hurried exit.

He saw Matt making his way towards him along the inner circle, and all Darkly could visualise was a huge explosion and a white mushroom-shaped cloud, and all that was left of Matt was a dark shadow on the tarmac of the pavement. Matt sat down and asked, "Have you got the tape with you?"

It suddenly shook him back to the business at hand. Should he tell Matt he had been in touch with one of the best computer brains in the country—if not beyond—and between them, they had worked out to extract the information on X15 and already had the information?

The disturbing part of listening to the heads of state again was they all agreed to instigate not a military strike, which had been the topic of the previous meeting, but an all-out nuclear attack, which would wipe out half the world's manufacturing. The estimate of civilians killed—or, more accurately, murdered—was not finalised.

"Yes, of course. It's here, Matt," Darkly said, fishing the case that contained the congealed silicon out of his pocket and holding it just out of reach of Matt, giving away none of the negative thoughts he had against Her Majesty's MI5 officers.

"Don't do anything hasty, Simon. We've got you covered from every angle."

"Why would you do that? What on earth do you think I'm going to do?"

"Can't be too careful in my game, Simon. Remember the warning from my boss at the last meeting. You must keep everything to yourself."

Darkly could have laughed, as it was obvious this was Matt's first big assignment they had trusted him with.

Darkly said, "Of course. I'm not stupid, Matt."

"We need to be able to trust you. I'll take the X15."

Darkly handed over the box containing the X15. The box itself was similar to a puncture-repair kit for a push bike, Darkly thought to himself with amusement.

Matt had checked the box and its contents before saying, "I hope I don't need to remind you, Knight, to remain on standby if we need you again. And if you breathe a word of this to anyone, you're a dead man walking."

He got up and, walking away, nodded into the distance and was gone. Darkly got his bike and rode off. London, like many major cities of the world, was now a slow-moving traffic jam, due to one-way streets with too many restrictions. He cycled back along Harley Street past the Fetal Medical Centre, towards Devonshire Street over Weymouth Street and out towards Cavendish Square Garden. He set off down Henrietta Place and took a left along the loop and Old Cavendish Street.

He could think clearly when he cycled, and he worked out his next move. He again visualised the white cloud produced by nuclear strikes and the utter chaos and death it would cause to innocent people. He must act decisively and fast. He started to work out his escape plan, what he would do if things fell apart and what he might do if they went well too.

Darkly crossed Oxford Street and on to Dering Street and through Hanover Square and Saville Row, round by Horse Guards along the back of Downing Street and in through the back entrance.

He made his way to his office, past all the banks of security cameras covering all aspects of Number 10 and also Downing Street itself, down to the metal gates which controlled all the coming and goings, past the main door entrance, and up to the other end.

CHAPTER 18

Darkly and Paul English made contact through Signal, which they knew would be secure.

Earlier, when Darkly had contacted Paul English after landing from his second visit to the George W Bush USA aircraft carrier, Paul had walked him through the way to set up his computer and listen to the recording from the X15. He had followed the instructions and got the shock of his life listening to the clear transcript. Events had moved on a pace since the last time. He now knew China and Russia had upped the odds by moving nuclear launchers into strategic positions. Had this been Ethan Miller's plan all along as Darkly had him down as an untrustworthy ally and thoroughly shady person?

Paul English's memos to Darkly had a particularly negative tone. He reviewed the reasons for not wanting to get involved any further—his family's safety, his pension, even his own safety. Were they bordering unlawful and even seditious activities, working against the government's wishes? However, each time Darkly put the true facts from the tape and explained the reasoning behind his own actions, he began to accept the argument. When Darkly explained something neither of them had anticipated—that the nuclear threat from both sides had been decided—Paul's decision had been immediate.

"Hi, Simon. I have to tell you that, against my better judgement, I am in!"

A sigh of relief emanated from Darkly's lips. He was happy they were typing to each other, and without any sound, the prof had no way of hearing the depth of Darkly's attitude.

"I will have written the first algorithms for the basic strategy shorty. These algorithms will run the virus, Simon. Luckily, it isn't term time, as I wouldn't have any time otherwise. I have not been so excited about any other project in years! The virus must be indestructible, easily divisible, and undetectable. I have ensured it lies dormant until it can move on. It doesn't have to be opened by the user, as it will travel. It constantly decrypts and edits its source code while constantly changing facilities. It is a persistent virus that will run in the background while remaining hidden. It will lie dormant in its host computer for a week before starting. I will transfer the virus onto a USB key. From there, you can start distribution. It is a nasty piece of work, Simon. Handle it carefully, won't you, my friend?"

"Christ, it sounds savage, Paul."

"Incidentally, the virus can be introduced to its host, through either their normal email or by using the USB. The latter you can use in Downing Street or any military HQ."

"Yes, I should be able to get access to GCHQ, which will cover this side of the pond. I can get good connections straight from Downing Street to the USA and the rest of the world. It'll take me some time, but two or three nights should be enough. I can also gain access to China and Russia, so we will have it all covered. I'll need three days to finish it. Jenny thinks I have a lover, by the way, because I am being so secretive and spending so little time at home."

He laughed at the idea and added this would cost him dearly; he hoped the ultimate fee wouldn't be the birth of another child. They both laughed, relieving the tension of such grim work.

CHAPTER 19

In the quiet of Chi Mou Yung's office, a nine-year-old boy sat on the shining wooden floor listening to his father.

"Now, my little Hai Nan, what have I told you about our people? How do we keep order?"

The small boy thought for some time.

"We keep them busy, Ba. Is that what you told me, Ba?"

"Yes, my little Hai Nan, I did say that. I also said we use something else to control the people."

We use *fear*, my little Hai Nan, fear. People of the West use the spectacles of religion and royal families and financial competition to keep their people in place. To keep theirs in order, Eastern leaders prefer violence, which, in turn, brings fear."

"How can you use fear, Ba?"

"Fear of being caught—like you when you know your mother is coming just when you are pulling the biscuit jar off the shelf," he said with a knowing smile.

"How did you know about that, Ba?"

"I know everything, my little Hai Nan—and in time, you must learn to know everything too."

"How do we learn everything, Ba."

"We get their friends, neighbours, or workmates to tell us."

"Why would they tell us, Ba?"

"Fear."

"Why do they have fear, Ba?"

"If they don't tell us, they fear we will separate their entire family, sending them all away to be retrained. Or, if we can't retrain them, we might send them to labour camps, where they will suffer inhuman brutality. If that doesn't work, we simply remove them. This is the way, my little Hai Nan. This is what they fear."

"When can I use fear, Ba?"

"At your age, you can use it in two ways. First, you can do better than your classmates—in your studies, for example. You can spend more time than they do making sure your learning work is perfect, and they will respect you and look up to you."

"I have to work harder at my studies, Ba?"

"Yes, always try to be one step ahead of everyone, Hai Nan."

"You said there were two ways to use fear, Ba?"

"At your age, the second way is to ensure they understand the position of your father."

"Is that you, Ba?"

"Yes, my little Hai Nan. That way, they will look up to you. That is enough for us today. Go to your mother, and tell her you are to receive a biscuit for listening well today. I have work to do with the Russian president."

The Chinese leader helped his son off the floor. They faced each other and bowed, each with his hands clasped together.

"Remember always: one day, you will take over my duties. By this time, we will have built a Chinese World Order. With our superiority in education and commerce, we will rule, and great responsibility will sit upon your shoulders. It is my life's work to ensure your shoulders are broad enough to carry this burden, my little Hai Nan."

The Chinese premier turned his attention to his screen.

The Russian and Chinese leaders had made initial phone contact to discuss their agenda. They used email to discuss matters they wished American hackers to read, aware that nuclear missiles travelled both ways.

***

Email from Mikhail Petrov to Chi Mou Yung:

To the Honourable Chi Mou Young,

We have obtained some valuable information from our security which will interest us both. This is the list sent by the US and UK. They are launching their attacks at bases around the Middle East.

We have identified the following targets: Shanghai, Beijing, Shenzhen, Hong Kong, North Korea, Chongjin Panchen, Pong Yang, Nampo Sari won, Russia, Moscow, Leningrad, Minsk, Safonov, Tergal, Norilsk, Novotroitsk, Ufa, Syzran, Dzershinsk, Vyborg. India, Chandrapur, Ludhiana, Bhiwandi, Vijayarranda, Firozabad, Panna Panipad, Bharuch Moradabad, Kanpur Varanasi, Surat, Pimpri Chinchwad, Tirupur, Chennai, Visakhapatnam, Byhalia, Jamshedpur, New Delhi, Mumbai, and Calcutta.

We must act swiftly. How do you feel about moving our mobile nuclear launchers into place as a deterrent?

Mikhail Petrov

***

Email from Chi Mou Lung to Mikhail Petrov:

This is moving very quickly. We have identified the same targets, but we need to slow down the entire campaign to allow us more time to move our mobile nuclear launchers.

It is interesting that the *West,* as they like to call themselves, have used military deterrents to keep the *East,* as they arrogantly call us, in check. The pendulum is now swinging the other way. It is now the East using nuclear deterrents to stop the West from killing millions of innocent people all over the world.

Chi

***

To the Honourable Chi Mou Young,

The one item we have been unable to determine is the date of the attack.

From the readiness of their attacks, we estimate we have approximately twenty days before they strike.

Let me know when you receive further information, and I will do the same.

Speak soon.

Regards,
Mikhail

CHAPTER 20

The normal sequence of seeing the wonderful person responsible for bringing Darkly up from age nine had gone by the board recently, which made it all the more enjoyable to amble down her short path, bordered with multiple varieties of forget-me-nots. The highgrove variety was at the front, in their white and grey splendour. Behind them were the pink ones—he couldn't remember their name—and then the darker blue Swarovski at the rear of the tiny, well-cared-for beds. He skirted around by the front door, past the brick chimney breast, and entered the garden through a small gate.

Immediately, Sadie bounded over towards him, tail wagging, snorting through her nose and shaking her head from side to side. He leaned down to give her a thorough petting, stroked her long coat, and kissed her on the top of her head as she whined and licked his hand. The golden retriever was a friendly breed, and since Auntie B retired, she had looked after Sadie like a second child. Auntie B had picked her as a puppy, and now she could spend more time walking and enjoying her company. Darkly went straight in through the back door.

"I'm home." His aunt's voice came from the direction of the front room to the left of the solid blue front door.

"Coming, Simon darling. Be there in a jiffy."

His Aunt Brenda came swiftly into the kitchen, flinging her arms around Darkly; he reciprocated and kissed her on her flushed cheeks. Although she was five feet, nine inches tall, her slim figure had to stretch up to kiss him back. They held onto each other a moment longer, and as she stood back, Brenda looked hard at him.

"So, what's kept you away for so long? It's not usually as long as this?" she said, pushing her neat brown hair away from her eyes.

"Oh, don't worry, Auntie B. I need to tell you a bit about what's cracking off at the moment anyway, but shall we decide what we're going to do today, and then I can tell you what I can as we go along."

"Yes, that's fine, Simon," she said with a smile. "It's the same as always—just like trying to get blood out of a stone. You've been the same since you were a child. I'll love you whatever, and you won't change now. To be honest, I had thought it could have been a young lady, but I get the feeling I'm way off track."

She looked inquiringly up into his soft grey-green eyes, noticing how much like his mother he looked.

Darkly laughed gently at this remarkable woman, who could read him like a book.

"OK, so, I'm guessing bees first and then lunch out and then what?" Darkly said.

"Yes and yes—and don't think you can get around me by taking me out to lunch. Mrs Hawkins next door will let Sadie out after lunch, so we needn't hurry," she said as she pushed him on the shoulder.

"OK, let's get togged up first. I'm guessing it's more frames. Do we need to make any up?"

"No, I've done that and got another super steamed and cleaned off."

"Perfect. Let's get started, then."

They locked the back door as they let themselves into the side door to the double brick garage. There, under a suspended blue cloth, stood Darkly's pride and joy. Darkly unhooked the rope off the wall and through the pulley, screwed into the centre of the cross beam of the pitched roof, and pulled the rope. It lifted off a large dust sheet, under which was a shining burgundy-red Bentley Continental. Darkly had researched the car, which was his boyhood fantasy. He had bought one that was fifteen years old. It hadn't belonged to a footballer, which meant it probably had not been driven fast, and even at that age, it had low mileage and was definitely garaged every night. The one he had found had cost under twenty grand and would have not been used every day. This one had travelled only 36,000 miles and had cost him £18,600. He had judged that a modern family sedan would cost the same and not be as much fun. Hand-stitched leather too! He had owned it for three years and enjoyed every mile.

"Leave that alone for the moment, Simon. You can take me to lunch in it. B's first," she said, brandishing the smoker at him jokingly as he put his hand on the wing.

"You know I would rather see you doing that to a young lady, Simon."

"I wouldn't possibly touch her there in front of you, Auntie B. Far too near to the engine!" he said, raising and lowering his eyebrows several times. They nearly fell over as they laughed.

"You know, Simon, when you first came to me, it took a full two years to get you to laugh like that."

"I'm sorry. I must have been hard work," he said, going over to her and putting his arm around her as she lit the dry old bark in the smoker.

"Not really. Tell you what, though, every page was worth turning."

She turned towards him, raising her voice as if she were getting the attention of a classroom of her kids.

"*Bees!*" she said as she lighted the dry bark, which began smoking profusely.

"Yes, marm," Darkly said with his tongue lolling out of the side of his mouth.

They both quickly donned their bee suits and checked each other over. They took the frames and the new super and the smoker puffing away down to near the bottom of her garden, passing as they did a tidy vegetable patch, bordered by raspberry bushes to one side and strawberry plants to the other; both sides had fresh straw carefully placed under all the ripening fruit. They came to a small enclosure on the left where the two national bee hives stood. They each took one hive. The smoker wasn't used much, especially as the bees were not aggressive and didn't need much calming down. They cracked open the layers as the bees filled any cracks with propolis, which was like a form of glue, used to make sure there were no draughts in the hive, as the queen needed to be kept warm all the time. Once open, they checked the individual frames to ensure there was no disease and whether the honey they produced had yet been capped, in which case, they could have taken away the frames and scraped off the honey. It was too early at this time of year for this by about two or three weeks. The honey was all stored on the comb, which the bees also made, by fanning the honey with their wings to evaporate the water, concentrating the honey. They also made the wax that capped it. They worked their way along with the supers. The one Darkly was tending needed the extra super Auntie B had prepared.

"Busy bees are happy bees," as Auntie B always reminded him.

"Where are we going this afternoon then?" he asked.

"Well, it's somewhere we haven't visited since you were a small boy, with your mum. It's near here."

"Ah, I won't get this right, but it's foreign sounding—and near Wimbledon Common? Italian, begins with K?"

"Cannizaro Park," Auntie B replied.

"Yes, I remember there was a rhyme you got me to say with you both."

Digging into the recesses of their memory, they both disjointedly began reciting the limerick.

There once was a count Cannizaro
Who went off to live with a young lady in Milano.
He never came back.
He had had some of that
Did that naughty Count Cannizaro.

"Wow, did we let you sing that?" she asked. "And yes, the count did go to Milan with a mistress and left his Scottish wife here on the estate. She carried on developing its unique and rare plants. There are even some seven hundred-year-old oak trees."

"I remember you two getting me to join you in the rhyme. I never did understand what he had had *some* of, but because you were laughing so much, I never asked. I do remember a lake, though."

"Oh, yes. Do you remember you wanted to go in for a swim on a particularly scorching day?"

"I remember you both laughing a lot when you were together."

"Well, what made us laugh then was because it was so hot, you wanted to swim in the lake, you had all but stripped off, and we had to tussle with you to keep your clothes on and not embarrass us. It was made worse by some people laughing at what you were obviously trying to do, and they egged you on."

"How many times do I have to apologize to you for my behaviour?"

"It wasn't that bad, really. Oh, look, the queen's here," she said, pointing at a bee much larger than the others, crawling across the other bees. Darkly looked over.

"She looks to be in a fine fettle, Auntie B. I couldn't see mine in the brood box."

This was a larger box at the bottom of the beehive and a wire mesh, which allowed the other bees to get into the supers above to make honey but kept the queen laying and germinating eggs, which would hatch in three to four days. They would then be fed by the worker bees. After that, they would go through several stages in the cells, which were capped when they pupated.

"Twenty-one days later, they emerge as worker bees, which are all female," she said.

Darkly said, "Well, I've put the new super in place, and I'm all done here, Auntie B, and feeling hungry."

"Yes, same here, Simon. Just need to pop the top on, and I'm finished and hungry too."

Darkly took the smoker across to the vegetable patch; he emptied the embers onto the bed of the bonfire area and joined his aunt in the garage.

"I'll wash my hands and get the Bentley out—if that's OK with you?"

"Yes, of course, Simon." She was out of her bee suit and looked back to Darkly. "I'll just need to freshen up and put some rouge on," she said, not taking her eyes off her nephew.

Darkly looked up in complete shock until he saw the glint in her eye and burst out laughing. "You got me, then. I thought I really had been away too long." He laughed so hard it took him a moment to catch his breath.

"Sorry, Simon, couldn't help it. Today has felt like we have slipped back thirty years. I'm only going to refresh my lipstick, dear."

Auntie B disappeared inti the house and upstairs, and Darkly made his way into the old pine kitchen, well in need of modernisation but immaculately clean and tidy, with a vase of roses in the window. He gave Sadie a bit more attention, washed his hands, and looked out onto the location of his happiest childhood memories. Birthday parties for him and his school chums, with the wind blowing the paper cups all over. The hot summers, with the hose running down a length of plastic; they would run and jump onto the plastic and slide all the way to the bottom. As the years rolled by, the girls would come and play with them too. His first kiss with Vivien Whitby. Those were the days. Look at what he had got himself caught up in now. He was working out how best and how little to tell his aunt. He had to think about her safety as well.

He had time to think about the white cloud following a nuclear explosion and the work he had to put in place to make things happen. He had a busy time ahead.

He collected his wallet and keys from his backpack and went out to the garage. The twin doors were the same colour as the front door; he unbolted and pushed hard as they caught on the drive. They opened to display the car of his dreams, an emblem of outstanding British engineering. He dropped the bottom bolts into the appropriate holes in the tarmac.

Darkly opened the driver's door and flipped the bonnet catch, went around to the front, pressed the safety catch, and lifted the bonnet. He checked the levels of the oil, water, brake fluid, and windscreen fluid. They were all OK. Even though he knew a light on the dash would tell him otherwise, he liked to check it himself. He let the bonnet click onto its closed position and wiped his hands on the rag under the front seat, replaced it, and glided into the driver's seat, electrically set to his safest, most comfortable driving position. He put the keys into the ignition and twisted. The six-litre engine almost silently vibrated rhythmically into action. He selected reverse and checked mirrors left and right, with the last check through the back window, and released the handbrake. Slowly taking pressure off the aluminium foot brake, it purred out of the garage onto the driveway. He braked the car and put the gear shift into park. Then he went and closed the garage doors and got back in the Bentley.

Auntie B came out, locked the back door, and came over to the passenger door, which Darkly leaned across and opened. She slid in and sank into the hand-stitched red leather passenger seat.

"Do you know it still smells of leather, just like it did when you first brought it?"

"Fantastic, isn't it? Still gives me the greatest joy every time I drive it. Right, off to the Royal Oak, then."

Darkly had been on any number of advanced driving courses, some of which had them hand-brake turning, changing direction, and any number of amazingly fast avoidance procedures, but Darkly drove the Bentley exactly to the speed limit, as though taking his test.

The Royal Oak had a good-sized car park, where they glided to a halt and got out. The old brick building had all the hallmarks of the coaching inn it had been used for before the advent of the motor car. They walked in through an archway with a rose bush trained around the edge, which was in full blossom. The smell was infectious, which probably sold the place before you even stepped through the door, Darkly thought. The coaches would have been driven through the arch into the courtyard to change their tired horses and for the travellers to get a bite to eat and throw down some weak local beer, which was safer to drink than the water supply. In the corner of the courtyard was a replica of an old coach. It was black with a red door.

"Did you know a coach like this would take nine paying passengers as well as the mail?" he asked his aunt.

"What a squeeze, Simon. I won't grumble anymore when I have to take the train," Auntie B said, laughing at the thought.

"Also, the driver sat on the right."

"Why was that, Simon?"

"Well, as most of us are right-handed, they held the whip in their right hand, and when they were getting the most out of the four horses, they didn't hit the passenger on their left. Also, they could draw a gun with their right hand."

"Yeah, got that. Is that why we drive from the right in the car?"

"Lots of theories, of course, but I think that's the most likely."

As they entered the old building, Darkly had to duck to miss hitting his head on the door lintel. They were shown to their reserved table by a short young man in a black suit. His hair was swept to one side over his right ear, and he had to flick his head back all the time to keep it in place. He was, however, extremely polite, albeit obviously new to the position of responsibility in which he found himself.

"May I take your drink order while you look at the menu?" he asked as he gave them their menus, which were printed on white paper and held in a folder which looked as though it could have been around when the inn was first built.

Darkly ordered his regular lime and soda, which he always drank, as he was a teetotaler, probably because of the way his father had abused alcohol and physically abused his wife, ruining the whole of Darkly and his mum's life, not to mention his own. Auntie B ordered a glass of Chardonnay.

As the young man went off to get their drinks, they looked at each other and smiled. Even his name badge had been put together without care. The G on Doug trailed off as though someone had been nudged when writing it onto the sticky label, which he wore on his jacket lapel.

"Do you remember your first job in the Rose and Crown, Simon? You were tongue-tied just like him. OK, a bit taller but overawed all the same."

Darkly shuddered at the thought. "Oh, yes, that first shift. Oh my, I thought I would die. I never thought I would get through it, and they had me shadowing Hettie Downs, who was two years above me at school. I was so embarrassed. I thought if only I could have disappeared through a hole in the carpet, and there were a few of those in the Rose!"

They both laughed, and then when Doug came back with their drinks, they thanked him and proceeded to order the same meals: homemade meat pies followed by sticky toffee pudding and custard.

Darkly brought up the subject of his own impending disappearance. He knew MI5 was paying him some attention. If his plan worked and he had to lie low and become invisible, Auntie B might be taken in for questioning, so the less she knew, the better. She had held a senior position in her state school, and he knew she had dealt with several male and female bullies over the years and could hold her own.

"Have you been involved in something you shouldn't have been, Simon?" she asked.

"Well, let me put it like this, Auntie B: if I give you the full knowledge about what I am doing, which I can't, you would approve. I have neither asked to be put in this position nor want to do what I am about to do. Honestly, the less you know now, the safer you will be. Will I need to make myself scarce soon? I think so. For how long? I really do not know. Should you worry? Negative."

"Well, now I'm more worried now than when you started."

"No need to be. Don't you trust me?"

"I have always trusted you. I do not want you to get hurt, darling—that's all."

"I will do my best to be in one piece the next time you see me."

Their meal was OK in the way modern pub meals are probably delivered to the pub and in frozen packs, and most will be popped in the microwave by staff who are not trained chefs and on low wages—and taste like it. They paid and left young Doug a decent tip. Darkly made his way back towards Wimbledon and Cannizaro Park. It was midweek, and they parked easily and strolled down the lines of geraniums and flocks towards the Roman pillars, which invited them time to circle around. All the time, Auntie B was trying to find a way to press Darkly for more information.

They approached the lake. The clouds made it a typical summer day—one minute very hot when the sky was clear, the next, cooler as the clouds obscured the sun, with occasional gusts of wind to rustle the grass. It was quiet where they were, and the bird songs were noticeably loud considering how near they were to Wimbledon itself, as Auntie B pointed out.

"It's so quiet because we have twelve acres to get lost in, which is a large piece of land. It's a bit smaller than George Harrison's."

"Where did that bit of information come from? Wait a minute, Auntie B. How do you know that about George Harrison?"

Auntie B pushed her hair, brown and flecked with grey, away from her eyes. Her slim figure and smooth skin made her appear much younger than she was. She rarely wore makeup, which gave her a beautiful natural glow. She had taken good care of herself, to the point where most people took her for Darkly's elder sister— much to their great amusement.

"He's dead now, of course, but you know how much I enjoy the Beatles' music. Well, I was reading an article about him and the Traveling Wilburys before he died. His house, Friar Park, at Henly, had sixty acres, and he wanted to put a lake on the grounds. He had to shift loads of earth, of course, but also the plumbing pipes for the house. Several large rocks needed to be moved, but he did it. The pictures made it look lovely, only the sort of thing rich people can afford. The Wilbury's all looked so happy when they were playing. They obviously enjoyed being together."

"Who looked so happy, Auntie B?"

"Oh, sorry, Simon—Bob Dylan, Roy Orbison, and Jeff Lynne … and George, of course. You know the Traveling Wilburys, dear."

Darkly looked at her and laughed. "I hadn't got you down as a groupie. So that's what's kept you busy all these years."

"Wouldn't you like to know Simon Knight," she said with a wicked smile.

Darkly put his arm around her and said, "Look, I may be away a whole year."

73

"Wow, you are into some serious stuff, Simon. Are you sure you're OK?"

"I'll make sure I'm safe—don't worry. The problem is I don't think I will be able to get in touch."

"Don't' like the sound of that one little bit," she said with a look of great worry on her face.

Darkly said, "The main reason I don't think I can get in touch is to keep my location totally secret."

As she led him away from the lake, she motioned for them to sit on a bench and turned to him.

"Don't you think I deserve a bit more than you're telling me, Simon?"

"Honestly, the more I tell you, the more I could put you at risk. Believe me, if I could tell you more, I would. Remember this: I love you with all my heart. I would not do anything unless it was necessary, and I am working to the good, whatever is said to you. Also, when it's finished, you are my first port of call."

"Keep safe, my lovely boy."

There was a tear in the corner of Auntie B's eye. Darkly leant closer and wiped it away. He hugged her for a long time, and when he released her, he said, "You know I owe you my whole life. You are the whole world to me."

Auntie B gave an involuntary sob and buried her head into his shoulder.

"You bloody soldiers," she said. She sort of sobbed again and then laughed. She turned to him and said, "But you know I like you," and she gave his shoulder a big thump.

"Blimey Dick Emery now, Auntie B." They both crumpled up in a fit of laughter.

Darkly wondered if life had always been like this when the men went off to war. The men were full of their future endeavour and enterprise, full of themselves, and eager to get on and leave the women to pick up all the emotional debris the men leave behind.

They arrived back at the house where the gates and doors were opened, and the Bentley carefully put under its cover. Darkly felt sad the way things had turned out and the way he had stumbled into the intel, which he could not ignore. His mind went to the white cloud which would kill all the innocents.

He collected Sadie from Mrs Hawkins next door and had a little chat about where they had been and what they had eaten. Also, she asked about Darkly's job and if he had met anyone important lately. Mrs Hawkins had a small veranda at the front of her bungalow, which caught the sun at this time of day, and they had sat on two wicker chairs with cushioned seats. Mrs Hawkins brought them out every day during the summer, and this was where much gossip was exchanged. She was a kind and thoughtful neighbour.

If a little lonely, Darkly thought. Her husband, Jack, had been a policeman, done his service, and retired here before his early death from a heart attack watching Arsenal. Quite understandable, really.

They heard Auntie B's voice from behind them.

"Hi, Jean. Thanks for looking after Sadie. Was she a good girl?"

"Oh, she's always easy to look after. Thanks, Brenda. I better let Simon go. I bet he's got to get back to Number 10."

Darkly brought Sadie in through the back door, gave her a last tussle and turned to his Aunt and kissed her on the cheek, hugged her, stepped back, picked up his backpack, turned and was out through the door and down the street towards the bus stop before Auntie B could collect herself. *Best way*, she thought. It meant she did not have any time to become emotional. She smelt her shoulder, which retained the faint smell of his aftershave and the smell of Darkly himself. She shuddered and closed her eyes. She went straight to her front room, picking up a biscuit for Sadie from the tin as she passed and poured herself a glass of very dry fine sherry. She picked up her mobile and dialled a stored number.

Auntie B said, "Hello, Jean. Simon's just left, and I'm just having a glass of sherry. Would you like to join me?"

"Thank you, dear. That does sound like a good idea. I'll be two shakes of a lamb's tail."

CHAPTER 21

The PM's phone rang.

"Good evening, Brett Caddick."

"Colonel Grant here, sir, GCHQ."

"Yes, Colonel, have you got an update for me?"

"Yes, sir. I'm sending an email with the Russian and Chinese movements. I'm afraid it doesn't make good reading, Prime Minister."

"OK, thanks, Colonel. I'll handle it from here."

"Right you are, sir. As we get more information, I'll let you have it immediately."

Brett Caddick read the email and found the whole of his body was shaking. He quickly stood up from his desk and bolted to his toilet, threw the seat up, and vomited into the bowl. Feeling terrible, he wiped his mouth with the linen handkerchief he always kept in this trouser pocket and looked at himself in the mirror. He wasn't up to this sort of pressure. The lines on his face seemed to have grown deeper, and the black rings under his eyes looked as if they had been painted on with a thick brush.

Sweat dripped off Brett Caddick's nose, and he used the same handkerchief he had used to wipe his mouth. It nearly made him wretch again because of the smell. He worked on the number of nuclear deterrents he needed to mobilise to keep in line with the guidelines put in place by US President Ethan Miller.

Including the submarines and different sites around the world and the targets they had established. He felt terrible, having not slept for the last few nights. His body ached as he went back to the schedule and started to make lists of the Chiefs of Staff he had to brief. He emailed Ethan Miller to keep him in the loop.

Almost immediately, the phone rang.

"Hi, Brett. Ethan here. From your email, I've had a look at the possible escalation and how quickly they can strike. We need to move straight away and bring our plan forward by several days."

"We can't, Ethan. It's not possible. I can't agree to go straight ahead with your plan."

"Our plan, Brett. Remember, we all signed up to this—you know we did. We don't have a choice, my friend. They know what we are up to, and if we don't move first, they will instigate our destruction, and we won't be alive to regret our delay."

"Look, there are bits I don't agree with."

"Too late we have to move now and plan to get our first strike in before they can get their units fully ready, and that is now, Brett. Look, I've got too much to do to start arguing at the last minute. Get it done, Brett, or you will have to pay for it. Speak to you later."

He abruptly stopped the call, and the line went dead. Brett wished it was he who was dead. He put his head between his hands and quietly wept. What could he do? If he did nothing, millions of innocent people might be slaughtered. But what were the alternatives? He could take his own life. Resign and be castigated as the PM with no backbone? He couldn't take his own life. He knew he was not man enough; that's what his wife always said to him. She said he never had the balls to do anything significant. The worst thing was he knew she was right.

CHAPTER 22

As soon as Darkly was back in Number 10, he shut himself in his office. He knew it would take hours to finish off the work he had started the night before, to get his USB into the contacts his computer had clearance for him to access. The lists were endless, and he kept adding to them all the time—politicians, heads of state, military units (air, sea, and land) and all the different departments, police, councils, embassies, energy departments, media outlets, overseas diplomatic agencies. There were then the manufacturing companies and so on. The list grew and grew. All were worldwide too.

He looked up at the clock, and it was now 2:30 in the morning. He felt his mind was exploding and that he was slowing down. The white cloud kept him thinking about the effects on all the populations. It also made him aware of how the dealings of some politicians had become corrupt and undemocratic, and decisions were made behind closed doors that were being made to support their own ends. The whole thing made him doubt the system. He had another sandwich. He had bought a supply, plus some cakes for the sugar from a local shop. Darkly had made lists of headings he needed to cover. He moved on to power supplies and utilities, leaving out water supplies. He finished those and moved on to media outlets.

Another three hours of hard work, in addition to the lack of sleep he'd gotten in the last two days, had started to take its toll. He looked out of the small window over the gardens at the back of the building and could see the faintest glimmer of daybreak showing through the clouds. The six-o'clock shift would be getting ready to start, and he wanted to be clear by then. He had already made up a bag for him to travel for later that day.

He was scheduled to escort Peter Newton, Deputy PM, to GCHQ at ten o'clock. He needed some final preparations to finalise before he started that journey. The virus had been designed by Paul English to lay dormant for seventy-two hours before it started wreaking havoc and destroying the hard drives of every computer it could work its way into.

By the start of the new working day, he was somewhere close. The virus had been sent out worldwide, and there was no going back. Ten o'clock had arrived. Darkly had managed a shower and smartened himself up to take Peter Newton to GCHQ.

Peter Newton had been especially quiet in the rear seat as they sped over to GCHQ. Keeping his nose stuck into his laptop. Darkly found he was like this with him normally, so he passed it off without further thought.

They arrived, and Peter Newton took off into the building. Darkly followed him in and asked to be able to use a computer. One of the secretaries took him to a quiet office with a selection of nine. He took his chance to get the USB in as many as possible. Peter Newton's time there was scheduled to finish soon as he had to get back for a meeting at number ten after lunch. Darkly made his way back to the car, and as he passed, the receptionist called him over.

She said, "Hello, are you Simon Knight?"

"Yes, I am."

"Message from Peter Newton to say he has been delayed and would you return to Number Ten on your own."

"Yes, that's fine. I'm on my way, thanks."

Darkly walked briskly over to the Black Range Rover and quickly took it out of the car park and onto the main road. Just out of sight of the security office, he floored the gas pedal and had the black beast roar down the A 40 towards London.

Darkly was aware that the last few days were make or break for the effective installation of the virus. As he drove, he went over the entire list. He had made to make sure he had overlooked nothing.

As he approached the outskirts of Oxford, the road changed from dual to single carriageway. He came scorching round a right-hand bend and noticed a black Audi being driven very fast following him.

He immediately took it as hostile and didn't waste any time making this big black 6-litre super car specially modified to cope with just this type of situation give a bit more to the pace.

The bullet broke through the rear window, making a noise like a thunderbolt, and he heard the spinning lead buzzed by his right ear before embedding itself into the windscreen support.

Assessing the situation, he surmised what calibre of bullet had been used, as anything bigger would have passed straight through the strut. It put him in danger which meant he had to react fast and with violence. It was his life against theirs, and he had been expecting something like this to happen.

Darkly spun the steering wheel heavily to the left, right foot off the gas, handbrake on as his right hand went to the door and pressed the button to take the driver door window down and at the same moment put his hand inside his jacket to his Browning, pulled it out of its holster and flicked the safety catch off. He had practised this procedure many times, and its effect was to confuse a following vehicle and bring your window round facing the opposite way.

The Range Rover spun on its axis, throwing up huge plumes of smoke from the screeching tyres as it lurched round one hundred and thirty-five degrees, bringing Darkly's window into full view of the Audi. The downside of this manoeuvre was that it slowed Darkly's vehicle down and gave an advantage to the Audi, which was charging down the road towards him, getting bigger and louder by the second. Darkly looked through their windscreen and could plainly see the faces of the two men in the front seats, took aim and released four rounds into the position of the driver. A red plume filled the driver's side of the car as it spun out of control, making dark skid marks on the tarmac as it careered off to the left of the road. Maintaining speed, it nosedived into a wide-girthed tree. Glass and metal flew everywhere, sending smoke and steam into the air as it ploughed into the tree, which lost half its length, the rear of the car upending and smashing the roof of the Audi into the tree. The remaining debris burst everywhere amid the crunching, grinding noise of the stricken vehicle. Darkly looked in his rear-view mirror as he released the hand brake, spinning the steering to the right as he floored the gas and resumed his progress towards London. As he straightened up and built up speed again one hundred yards away, a blue Audi handbraked and, spinning sideways, came to a stop facing him broadside across his own path.

To his left were the large established trees he wanted to miss. To his right was a ditch which gave him the choice of doing a 180. He chose the latter, and as he was going through the right angle, off to the right-hand side of the road, he noticed there was a raised bridge made up of earth which would give access for a tractor and trailer to go through a gate leading to a field. The gate was closed and old. Darkly whipped the wheel to the left and flew over the earth bridge, smashing through the gate and into the field. The blue Audi was facing the other way, which gave him a time advantage, albeit a small one—enough time to steer around a copse to his left, throwing up grass and earth as the heavy car fought for grip on the soft surface. He got around the copse and was heading back to the gate when he heard from his right the revving engine of the Audi fighting for purchase as it sped towards the gate. He pulled the wheel hard to the left and lost control as the car lurched onto a foot-deep rut in the field, nearly rolling it over, and shot him into the thicket, where he managed to come to an abrupt halt. The Audi, meanwhile, having flown through the gate, was now in the field. Darkly's position, being lower, was hidden behind the trees, which gave him the chance to take aim and release several rounds into the inside of the vehicle. The Audi lost control, spun to the left, and rolled over twice, coming to a halt on its side. Darkly opened his door, and as he ran through the trees towards the Audi, it gave him the time to drop the spent magazine from his gun and reload.

He could see through the windscreen three occupants were dead, and a fourth, in the back seat, was undoing his seat belt. Darkly double-tapped him in the head and another double-tap into the chest. He recognised the man from his meeting in the café. This guy had been one of the heavies. There was movement from the gate as another figure ran into the field; Darkly quickly realised this one must have been flung from the other car during the crash, pulling his Browning out of its holster, levelling the barrel at Darkly, and firing. Darkly had seen the intension and bent his knees and leaned back hard just as the bullet buzzed by his shoulder, splitting the fabric of his suit as it went. In three huge strides, Darkly was over to the figure and kicked the gun out of his hand and threw his fist hard into his throat. Deputy Prime Minister Peter Newton staggered back, clutching his throat, and gasped.

"Knight, we have to talk. PM Caddick has resigned, and I am to take over. This is my chance. You have to stop whatever it is you're doing. I can't let you spoil this chance for me. You've got to understand."

Darkly thought back to his time in Afghanistan. He had never felt close to Newton. Even after the rescue, Newton had distanced himself during the rest of their tour. It became worse once they were both working at Number 10. Newton had cold-shouldered him.

Darkly knew he was fitter, stronger, taller and better than Newton in close unarmed combat. He wasn't going to shoot him in cold blood.

Darkly said, "How many will die then?"

The sun shone through the branches of the trees, which were casting shadows all around them, Darkly was able to see the flash of the blade as Newton shot his arm forward, going for a straight throat jab. He flexed his knees and leaned away as fast and far as he was able and managed to give him fresh air and kicked hard in a sideways motion right into Newton's knee joint, which made Newton howl. It looked like he may have broken the joint. Darkly remembered that his adversary was good with a knife. The resulting slash upwards cut Darkly's sleeve up to the elbow. Newton thought he had cut him, and he looked down expectantly, hoping to see the spurt of an artery. That instant of hesitation cost him his advantage. Darkly kicked his right knee again as Newton let out a cry of agony and collapsed on that side. As he put his hand down to the pain, Darkly took his advantage, stamped on his hand and grabbed him under the chin pulling his head up and smashed him hard in his temple. Newton collapsed onto the grass unconscious. He really couldn't kill him even though he was an evil bastard.

He realised the carnage he had already caused caused changed the whole balance for Darkly. The British establishment now considered him a wanted man.

CHAPTER 23

Darkly had to move fast, as he could visualise the white mushroom of complete destruction. He must only focus on his plan. Darkly scanned around for any unwanted company and breathed a sigh of relief as he saw no one. It was clear. He ran back to the Range Rover, flicking the automatic rear door opener as he went. He took out his bike and backpack, the latter he threw onto his back. The primary objective was to leave no trace and vacate the site fast. He chose to get to the edge of the field and go round two sides in case anyone showed up he could disappear into the foliage. He aimed for a gate at the opposite side.

As he was approaching the gate, his breath was thick and fast, and he needed to regain his equilibrium. He took three deep breaths, held his breath for two seconds, and let the air out slowly. It immediately reduced his diaphragm from pumping hard up and down. He threw the bike over the gate, broke its fall to stop any damage, and followed himself, throwing his abdomen onto the top of the gate, throwing his legs over and grabbing the middle spar so that he landed on his feet. He took one last look around and immediately got out of view. He cycled away hard to create distance, knowing they would not expect him to be on a bike.

He needed to get his bearings. Within half a mile, he found a track heading towards the north. He took it, pulling off into a small clearing that appeared on his left. He ripped off his clothing, storing his suit in an elasticated compartment on the side of his backpack so he could ditch it in a trash can later where it would never be looked for, nor found, and put on his cycling gear and helmet. He had planned the route and needed to set off. RAF Croughton lay due north from his position, and he could afford to follow that setting for an hour and then go onto sat nav on his mobile.

Two nights earlier, Darkly had spoken to Sergeant Darren Foster, Jane's twin brother. He was stationed at USAF Lakenheath and expressed the need for secrecy, and set up a get out of gaol plan. Darren had told Darkly to get to RAF Croughton and report to US Sergeant Keifer Ballantine, he would be put on a 2130 hours US Air Force Chinook helicopter flight to Lakenheath, where Darren would meet him. The flight would take less than one hour, and there, would be a US troop and equipment cargo 707 flight, ETD 2300 hours, to the States.

It was now 1930 hours, and the 20-mile cycle should take just under two hours. Could he make that in time in the dark. It was just possible if he did not have any distractions. He also needed to make the journey without being seen, as he didn't want a reception at the US end except for Jane.

It meant he had to travel off-road as much as possible, as he was now a wanted man probably being hunted by the police as well as MI5. Anyone trying to find him would probably go south to London. He looked at his watch compass and thought for the first hour it would be safe to follow his plan and head north using off-road tracks and as planned, he could use his sat-nav to RAF Croughton. He put in a bit more effort than his normal speed. He had got a long spell during two flights to rest, so two hours of exertion now was his target.

As the dimming daylight left him to get accustomed to the gloom and had to use his own lights. He was making good time, about forty minutes in when a large wooden object thrown from the right-hand side of the track hit him on the shoulder. He looked to his right and could make out some movement but could not pull the bike back from a heavy swerve which resulted in him coming down sideways. As he came to a halt, he stepped off the bike and looked behind him. There were three large men running fast to catch him up, and he only had seconds to react and work out how to extricate himself from this position quickly. He would surprise them with a frontal attack and lay them out where they stood. It had to be fast as he couldn't afford to lose any time at all.

Just as they were nearly on him, he shouted to them to stop or they would get hurt. They ignored the warning and laughed. He shot to his feet, sprinting towards them. He took the largest out first with a straight fist to the throat. He then ducted, and as he straightened up, he swung his left fist hard, grinding it into the skull of the guy on his left just below the ear. He joined his mate on the track. As Darkly turned to face his third assailant, he noticed in the little light left, the reflection from the blade of a knife which was aimed mid-body. Without losing pace, Darkly took his assailant's wrist, which was holding the knife, and swung around and kicked his feet from under him, dislocated his arm and to make sure, broke it by kicking hard at his elbow. He was groaning with the pain in his arm and was lying on his side. Darkly kicked the knife into the shrubbery, and gave him a sharp fist into the side of his temple, which would put him out for enough time for Darkly to escape. He made sure they were all breathing; he did not want any more unnecessary deaths. Although he could ill afford the time he decided to go through their pockets for any mobiles. They each had one and he threw them as hard as he could away from the track. They were unlikely to go to the Police as they looked like travelers. He would be well gone by the time they came round and be able to summon any help.

Darkly checked his bike over and resumed his passage. He had lost at least five minutes, presuming they would have robbed him except that they had been unlucky in the choice of their victim.

The white cloud was in the corner of his mind. He was chasing forward to stop it happening. He increased his speed and knew he had to get away from this area fast. Twenty minutes later Darkly pulled up to set up his sat-nav. He had fifteen miles to cover in the last hour and most of it would be off-road. He set off knowing it would be close. He covered the final fifteen miles in fifty minutes, feeling his cycling shirt wringing wet from the exertion, and out of breath.

He approached the red and white barrier to RAF Croughton

and two US privates approached him. One held his bike as the other checked his name against their list.

"So you are Sergeant Knight. Could you wait a second I'll get Sergeant Ballantine." A phone call was made, and the door from the gate house swung open and a tall, black man probably in his fifties with greying temples smiling all over his friendly face, stepping quickly over and shook Darkly by the hand.

"Thought you weren't going to make it. My Jeep's here. We'll save time, and I'll run you over to the Chinook myself."

"Thanks, Sergeant. Bit of a close call."

They swung the bike onto the back seat, and Sergeant Ballantine floored the gas pedal. They roared up the central driveway and over to where the final items were being loaded onto the huge rear door of the Chinook. Darkly's bike was taken off him and wheeled up the slope, then strapped to the inside of the fuselage.

The blades of the Chinook started to rotate. Sergeant Ballantine spoke to the floor manager, who nodded at Darkly. The sergeant came over to Darkly and shook his hand again.

"Have a good journey, Sergeant."

He gave Darkly a plastic sachet containing a pair of earplugs, which he gladly took. Sergeant Ballantine walked down the ramp, and as he looked over his shouldr Darkly was able to wave as a sign of thanks, Ballantine waved back and stepped off as it started to close, and they lifted off the ground. Darkly gave a sigh of relief and settled into the uncomfortable seat for the short journey to Lakenheath. The first part of a long journey began.

The Chinook gently settled on the tarmac at RAF Lakenheath. Immediately, the huge rear ramp began opening, and the military personnel unbuckled their belts, preparing to disembark. The corporal specialist first-class had unhooked Darkly's bike and was looking around for him.

"Thanks, Corporal. I'll take it from here."

"You're welcome, sir. You would be surprised how many items have got left behind when the staff are flying back home, now we always have to clear the decks. Have a good ongoing flight, sir.

"Thanks again, Corporal."

As Darkly reached the bottom of the ramp, a tall, slim, blond E 9 specialist Master Sergeant stepped forward with a smile and his hand outstretched.

Darkly had to swap hands so his bike wouldn't fall over

"Welcome to USAF, Lackenheath Darkly."

"Good to meet you in person, Darren." Darkly took a look at the chief master sergeant.

"I hadn't expected you to be so tall."

"Yeah, I got all the height and Jane got all the brains. Yeah, we kid my mum that we've got different fathers."

They both laughed.

"Listen in, quick serious note Darkly: you are not officially booked on the flight from Lakenheath, which is what you asked me to do, right? As soon as you step on the aircraft, you are on US of A turf, and I've got you a seat reserved. You won't have to show any papers at the other end. You'll be travelling as my guest. They be a won't be able to trace you, OK?"

"Can't thank you enough, Darren."

"Only payment is to look after my lovely sister. I've got two months' leave owing. I'll be over in the States and look you up?"

"Great. I will still need to be under the radar. So, for their own safety, even your parents won't know where we are. When I am in the States, I will give Jane a mobile, and either of you can contact me on that."

"Shit, Darkly, you are very organised. What have you been up to?"

Before Darkly had time to reply, they were walking towards the huge opening at the rear of the fuselage of the 707 cargo plane. Chief Master Sergeant Foster called out to the group of air force personnel on the tarmac.

"Privates Stilo and Koplinsky."

"Yes, Sergeant."

"I want this guest of mine looked after like royalty. You're both on the flight?"

"Yes, sir, we are," replied Private Stilo.

"OK, good, Stilo. Show the sergeant to the seat I booked for him under my name, understood?"

"Yes, sir."

"Kaplinsky, take the bike, and make sure the sergeant gets it back the minute you touch down in the States. Yes?"

"Yes, sir."

Darren turned to Darkly.

"Have a good flight. Look after Jane, and I'll see you within months. You can tell me all then."

Darkly said, "Yes, will do, and again, many thanks, Darren."

Darren patted him on the shoulder and walked away.

Private Kaplinsky took his bike off, and Darkly went with Private Stilo up the steps to the seated area in the plane.

Within two days, his virus would start its work, devastating computers worldwide. The main targets were government, military, media and television, manufacturing and transport, wholesaling and air travel. He had tried to keep clear of all medical and educational facilities. He could not guarantee where it would stop. The primary target was to stop the unnecessary killing of millions of innocent people throughout the world from nuclear destruction.

How much of his future would Jane want to be involved in? Would he ever be free? Could he be caught? Would a welcoming committee arrest him and deport him to the UK, where he might spend the rest of his days in gaol? He had no answer to any of these questions. He just hoped MI5 was still looking for him over there, not realising he had managed to escape across the pond, but for now, he must not be found. He would meet Jane and let her make up her own mind. Would she want to disappear with him and allow him to use all his skills to lie low? He must disappear without a trace, with or without Jane. He settled back in the business-class seat, looking towards an uncertain and chaotic future.

CHAPTER 24

E-7 Chief Petty Officer Jane Foster had worked her way up from E1 trainee seaman. She wanted to start at the lowest rank to gain respect later in her career. The recruitment officers told her it was unnecessary in today's US Navy. She stuck to her guns, started at the bottom, and enjoyed every minute. It really meant something to be in the largest and most powerful navy in the world. As she progressed through each position, she had learnt about the ranks and what part they each played. Jane had learnt all the knots what part they all played as they came into port and came alongside other vessels. She worked on the bridge and boiler room; in weapons deployment, catering, medical, and navigation. At each new task, she had felt comfortable with other personnel. She had not experienced the sideways glance from subordinate crewmembers who thought she had started above them. Jane enjoyed the friends she made along the way. Male or female, she made no distinction. She had set a rule that she would not date any navy rankings at all under any circumstances.

The other exciting part of being in the US Navy were the different places she visited. Some were areas of conflict, and other deployments were for humanitarian welfare. Wherever Jane travelled, she came across friends she had made during her years in the service.

She took all the various opportunities to study and take advancement and had recently made chief petty officer. The afternoon when she first met Darkly, their duties were to welcome foreign leaders and their security staff. Jane's brief was to escort the British prime minister's security people onto the ship, show them where the cabin and eating facilities were, and escort them to the wardroom where the main meeting would occur the following day.

Jane got the shock of her life when this dark-haired, handsome, fit-looking, tall man stepped down from the RAF F-35 onto the deck, looked around, and headed straight towards her with a smile and presence that weakened her at the knees. She looked into his eyes as he stretched down to shake her hand. She felt something stir deep within her she had never felt before. She found his accent irresistible and knew she had been smitten.

She remembered this happened to her mother when she had first met her father and that they had all laughed and said that it was not possible, and here she was, falling under the same spell, as though it was in her genes. As she showed this complete hunk of a man around the ship, she tried to stay more focussed and keep her mind on the job at hand. Jane realised that the thoughts going through her mind were forbidden and would be perceived as dereliction of duty and would be punished by dishonourable discharge. The years she had worked so hard to get where she had, and yet here she was, contemplating putting her future in the navy in a position of extreme risk.

These thoughts were churning through her mind as they had innocently entered his cabin. Somehow they had touched, and sparks had flown. A fire had been ignited. Neither of them had much control over it at all or even expected it to happen, the full force of which had bound them together. They'd thrown caution to the wind, and after which, they had both felt happier than ever before, knowing that at that time and place, they could be forgiven for not doing the correct thing, even taking into account the possible consequences.

Jane had been waiting for the flight to arrive at the McGuire Air Force Base. She had walked down with the other expectant relatives and friends onto the tarmac. Facing into the wind, she felt the fresh air in her face, threw her head back, and shook her head to straighten the long dark brown strands.

Darren had phoned her the night before to give her the base and time of the flight he had personally put Darkly on. She felt nervous and didn't want her hands to start sweating. She took three long, deep breaths and exhaled slowly to decrease her heartbeat and lower her blood pressure. She didn't want to be all hot and flustered when Darkly arrived.

She could hear the noise of the crowd changed as they looked towards a small silver dot on the horizon. They pointed as it grew bigger. The engine jets could then be heard whining as it slowed down for its final approach. They had been marshalled into a safe but close area on the runway, which meant the plane touched down some way to the right amid smoke and screeching tyres as it thundered towards them in a shimmering image spewing out dust and heat with the engines changing their note to an even higher scream. Jane realised that none of this could normally be seen or heard or smelt from the departure lounges into which the public was allowed.

Finally coming to a halt in front of them, a wind wafted past them, full of distinctive aeroplane fuel and the dust of flight and heat. You knew from that smell you could be nowhere else but an airfield.

Immediately, the side and rear doors were opened, the steps were wheeled into position, and personnel stepped onto the tarmac, some intent on further travail, others looking around for that person they longed to see and hold. Jane was so absorbed in this process that she jumped when a voice, distinctive but with an accent she could not place.

"Jane, I'm here. They let us out from the other side of the plane."

She threw her arms around his neck and kissed him with the fury and passion of months of anticipation.

"Sergeant, your bike's here, sir."

They withdrew from each other to turn to be presented with Darkly's bike, as promised by her brother Darren.

"Thank you, Private Kaplinsky. I appreciate that."

"You're welcome, Sergeant."

All delivered in the best Montanan accent Darkly could muster.

Private Kaplinsky frowned and then smiled, winked, and smartly turned on his heel and walked away.

"Wait a minute, Sergeant Knight. Are you having fun with me? What's with the American accent and all?"

"Jane, I have a long story to tell you. At this point, I don't want anyone to think I'm anything other than an average normal American guy meeting his girl. I've got three passports in my backpack, a bundle of cash, and a plan. I need about two hours to try to explain to you what's happened in my life since I first met you. Maybe a meal somewhere decent, as I'm starving. I'll pay."

"Well, as I've taken a month's leave vacation, I'll let you buy me lunch."

They walked and talked about the journey and Darren's help, which made it all happen, Darkly pushing his bike towards the car park. When they reached Jane's very second-hand pick-up, he put the bike in the back and got in the driver's side. A cough from Jane had him sliding across to the passenger side.

"Guess I'll have to get used to your English habits," she said with a laugh.

"Yes, sorry, I wasn't thinking. I think I'm a bit tired from the journey, and the last few days have been a bit hectic, as you'll find out."

Jane had made her way out of the car park, and it was another eight minutes before they were outside McGuire Air Force Base. She had already googled a restaurant and set up the sat-nav to take them straight there.

"So, come on, what's with the Montanan accent?"

"OK, so your brother was good enough to take me at my word and get me on the flight under another name. I have arrived here, and no one knows I'm here. That will become more understandable as the story unfolds."

"You betcha, Darkly. The more I hear, the less I like it, to be quite honest."

Darkly knew he could not have told her the story before he came over to the States. He had thought it through many times, and apart from the lack of security, because you would never know who might be listening, especially as he knew he was being scrutinised by MI5, but how do you tell a story to someone you feel you have fallen in love with, whom you don't know well at all, and who is fixed on a career in the US Navy? This was already looking as though it might be going badly, he thought, but he had to press on. Get it all out now and take the consequences.

They arrived at the restaurant, which was quite upmarket. Jane parked as far away from the main entrance as possible so no one would judge them on the age of the vehicle.

They were seated at a good table in a quiet part of the restaurant. They ordered drinks and starters.

Darkly had started by telling her that the scientific work going on in the States showed that from that date, the earth had six months within which to act and stop pollution.

Their starter course arrived.

If pollution did not stop, the rate at which the earth would heat up would be exponential. The earth would start to heat up at such a rate it could not be reversed. In two years from that date, man would be unable to survive the extreme temperatures.

They ordered their main course. Jane looked uneasy.

He told her about MI5, asking him to trial a new listening device. He had agreed, although he could never have known the result. When he listened to the tape, he had overheard part of the content of the meeting in the North Atlantic, when they had first met, how MI5 had asked him to be involved through the prime minister, and they were the ones who wanted him now. They wanted him dead, to be more accurate. At that time, because of the poor recording, he had thought that the US president wanted to use military strikes to take out all the highly populated areas as well as all the manufacturing plants producing the pollution, mainly in the Southern Hemisphere.

Their main course arrived. Darkly judged that Jane now looked angry.

Darkly went over the second meeting and that the president hadn't wanted to strike these areas with military weapons but use *nuclear* instead. Many millions of innocent people would lose their lives. It was unthinkable anyone would agree to use nuclear weapons. It was at this point that he told her about his old mate who was now a professor at the university where they had both studied and shared a house. Between them, they had designed a computer virus and executed its introduction throughout as many world outlets as was possible.

The virus would start its action within the next couple of days. It was designed to stop the whole of the world's computer networks from launching nuclear weapons. He recalled the trip to GCHQ and the number of agents he had to kill to stay alive and the deputy PM, whose life he had saved once in Afghanistan and then spared only yesterday, even though he had been trying to kill Darkly at the time.

It was at this last part of his story that Jane pushed her plate to one side, and, red-faced, told him that she had heard him through. It was the biggest pack of lies and made up nonsense she had ever had the misfortune to have to listen to. She had her career in the US Navy to think about, and she could not have anything to do with him ever again. He was a danger to everybody, including himself, and she suggested he get himself and his three passports and his false accent back to England and get booked into a clinic. She did not want to have anything more to do with him.

She got up from the table, told him not to follow her, and walked straight out of the restaurant.

Darkly sat still for a few minutes, trying to absorb what had just happened, how he had got this so horribly wrong. He wanted to shout after her that she had misunderstood and did not comprehend what was at stake. He motioned to the waiter.

"Everything OK with you guys?"

"Yeah, we're good, thanks. I'll pay the tab."

Darkly paid the bill and left a good tip. He walked out to the car park and saw that Jane had offloaded his bike onto the spot where her pickup had been parked. She had disappeared. He felt dazed, tired, and miserable. How had he got this so terribly wrong? He felt strongly towards Jan and thought it was reciprocated, that she would give him a fair hearing. He knew he was not experienced with women, especially in matters of the heart. He had thought like a man, and what he had told her was not what Jane would have wanted to hear.

He had already set out a second plan in case something like this occurred and things went wrong. He first found the nearest train station and boarded a local train to New Brunswick. From there, he could get a train to Seattle in Washington state, on the West Coast. As the train progressed towards New York, he went over all the eventualities. The worst was that he had the whole of the USA military after him. Could Jane have misunderstood what he had told her? Was the story true or realistic? He knew it was but realised it was too much to take in; he had expected too much from Jane and from a man who she did not know too well.

The train pulled into New Brunswick Station, its wheels screeching as it came to a halt. The noise brought Darkly round from the half slumber he had let himself float into. Everyone seemed to be in such a rush. Darkly could feel the heat of the day and the smell of train stations the world over. He let the crowds race off to their destinations and looked for somewhere to rest and make the reservations he needed. He found he could not get booked onto a sleeper that day and that he could reserve one for the following day, which left at three in the afternoon.

He had jettisoned his old phone before setting off to RAF Croughton. As soon as he was in the US, he bought another pay-as-you-go phone so he could not be tracked. He used the phone to find a hotel. The Western Plus Hotel, with its three-star US rating, would give him the quiet he needed at a reasonable price.

He made his way towards it, realising that, possibly within hours, all these systems might not work anymore after the world's computers stopped working due to his virus. The reaction he received from Jane had made him doubt his own actions. Did he have the right to have taken this whole agenda into his hands? Were he and Paul English now enemies of the state, despised and hunted across entire continents?

"By strength and guile" was the SBS motto, and it was how they had approached this, and he knew he had to follow it through to the end. He checked into the hotel and used cash and the American passport he had acquired as his ID. It was quite a smart hotel and even had a swimming pool, which Darkly knew he wouldn't have time for.

"You come for Mr Vaughan?"

"Yeah, just flown in and need some sleep."

"OK, got that, sir. A nice quiet room for you: 312. Take the lift to the third floor and turn left. Do you need any food, room service, or bellhop, Mr Vaughan?"

"No, I'm good, thanks. I just need to get my head down, thanks."

"We are all good here, sir. You have a good stay."

"Thanks."

Darkly made his way up to the room and was pleased to see a double bed.

Could he be traced? As he had binned his old sim card and then trashed his old mobile on his way to RAF Croughton. He was travelling on a genuine US passport and using cash. He bought a new phone on his way to the hotel so it would be difficult to trace. His accent had been good enough to pass him off as an American travelling through. Would Jane shop him? He really couldn't be sure. So many doubts in his head, yet he knew it made sense to follow the original plan. Follow it to the letter.

Darkly stripped off and took a hot shower, taking his time to relax and feel clean. It might be his last one for several days. He dried off, checked everything was off and the "Do not disturb" sign was on the door, closed the curtains, crawled under the duvet, and fell straight to sleep.

Ten hours later, the bedside phone rang. Groggily he picked up the receiver.

"Reception here, Mr Vaughan. We have a lady who says she is a friend of yours, Jane Fraser, but she didn't know your name or room number. I won't put her through unless you're OK with taking the call. Sir, she was very insistent."

"Yes, that's fine. You can put her through, thanks."

"You're welcome, Mr Vaughan. I'm putting the call through now, sir."

What did Jane want? How had she found him? He was sure Jane didn't want anything to do with him. He had blown the relationship even before it had begun.

"Darkly?"

"Yes, it's me, Jane. How the hell did you find me?"

"US Navy training. Put yourself in the shoes of the other guy. what would I do if I were you? Well, first, I thought you might use cross country flights. Those lead nowhere. Then I thought—"

"Wait a minute, Jane, are you keeping me on the phone so the FBI can storm my room?"

Darkly shot out of bed, threw down the phone, and raced towards his backpack and clothes. He opened the room door and looked up and down the corridor. He picked up the phone again.

"You still there?"

"Yes, I, am Darkly. I'm on your side. Incidentally, so is Darren."

"What are you saying? What do you mean?" His mind became clearer as he shrugged off the sleep.

"For one thing, Darkly bloody Knight, I'm a bit more difficult to get rid of than you might think. Secondly, I have a brother who can find out about just about anything." Jane's voice was rising in volume.

"OK, OK, cool down, Jane. What do you mean when you say you're on my side?"

"When I left you, I was so angry at the unlikely story you told me, I had to pull off the freeway and think and keep calm. So, of course, I phoned Darren, who had just got up, and he said that on the UK news, they reported a massive cyberattack overnight and that government military installations were at risk from the attack, which they warned was ongoing, and could escalate to communications all over the country. So, Darren made a few calls and found out that the US military had been recalled and put on nuclear attack mode. US nuclear submarines had been put on alert and were awaiting further instructions. The USAF had received similar briefs to equip bombers with nuclear missiles."

"Jesus Christ."

"Darren's intel matched exactly with what you said. That is when I realised I had to find you to tell you I love you and believe every word you told me. I still have a month's leave to take, preferably with you."

"Wow, some turnaround. How the hell did you find me then?"

"Well, I got nowhere with the airlines. I thought they were too open for someone who wanted to disappear. That's when I wrote down where you were at. You were tired. You would have wanted to get the hell away from where I last saw you. So, I went for west and north. How to achieve that? By rail. So I thought Mr cool dude would sit tight and stay low and get some shut-eye. Where? A hostel would be too noisy, and I knew you had money, hence my phone calls to hotels. Some wouldn't speak to me, the posh ones. Then I thought deeper and came up with the fact you would have chosen a decent hotel so you could sleep, and I could say I met you on a flight and you were from Montana knew my name although I didn't know yours, and of course, I knew your description."

"Well, you could knock me over with a feather."

They both laughed.

"Wait till I tell Darren I've found you."

"Good old Darren. He really helped me."

"He helped both of us."

"If you are you going to contact him, It would be essential for him to be able to find us."

"How do you mean?"

"Communications are going to go down worldwide. I told Darren I would have a non-traceable mobile so you can phone me when communications are up and running again.

"Wait a minute, buster, I haven't come all this way to left outside your hotel till it goes light again."

"What did you say? I don't quite follow. Ah, this is when the FBI breaks down my hotel room door?"

"Do you want to meet me in reception, Darkly?"

Darkly didn't take the lift. Instead, he bounded down the fire escape stairs two at a time, holding onto the bannister as he made it around the corners down one floor, then the second, and finally the third, falling through the swing doors and nearly stumbling into the reception area.

It was a large area, with many people meeting their colleagues or friends, and it went unnoticed as they threw themselves at each other and Darkly held Jane off the carpet.

"I really thought I had lost you, Jane."

"You very nearly did, you big oaf. Next time you have something important to share, give it me indigestible bits I can take in."

They had got in a lift, and it was whisking them silently up to the third floor. Darkly had taken Jane's small case off her and was holding her around the waist as she was holding him around the neck, not taking her eyes off him.

They got through the door to their room and somehow managed to undress in the few strides it took to dive onto the bed and enjoy each other's bodies touching each other's sensitive parts and finally amid the intake of breath and groans, moans and a heart-thumping atomic explosion of one glorious fulfilling moment together.

CHAPTER 25

George Henry Smith was ushered into the prime minister's office. There is a desk facing the window overlooking the half-acre of gardens at Number 10. The spring flowers had just finished, the early blossoms of summer were emerging, and the insects were getting busy. The trees all had their leaves except for the ash, which was always late.

Normally Brett Caddick would expound his knowledge of horticulture, but today, he was serious and got straight down to business.

"Good afternoon, GH. Please, sit down. We have something I would like you to take on board. Our conversation must remain confidential to all except your own people. I have something delicate to discuss, and for reasons which will become obvious, I am only able to fully trust SIS. MI5 are too busy with internal defence and terrorist threats. I can't trust the Met or anyone here. Also, I find you easier to talk to."

"Kind of you to say so, Prime Minister."

"Yes, well. This is the problem. Over the last six years since I've been PM, I've noticed huge sums of money disappearing. At first, when the sums were smaller—a little amount here, a small figure there—I thought it might have been too many consultants or outsourced contracts, but as the overall figure increased, I realised there was a serious problem, and I was the only person who could see the full picture. Over the six years, the total has amounted to £760,000,000."

He looked up to see GH's brown eyes widen in disbelief.

"When you say, 'money disappearing', what do you mean, Prime Minister?"

Brett Caddick bent towards a lower drawer on his beautifully polished mahogany desk, opened it, and took out a small blue hardbacked notebook. He flipped through it, found the page he wanted, and held it open with his thumb.

"Yes, good question, GH." He read from his handwritten notes.

"Fifty million pounds put aside for a new factory and manufacturing unit and development in the north-east, nothing happened; £76 million ring-fenced for a climate change survey, nothing; £35 million feasibility study for redesigning northern town centres; £94 million for Black Lives Matter, social education, and employment fast-tracking for minority groups, gone completely quiet. During Covid, I haven't obtained all the figures, but it currently runs at £135 million and counting. Need I go on? None of it has actually happened. All, on the face of it, are good, worthwhile projects. The papers pick up on a story, but the rest gets forgotten, and the longer it runs, the deeper it is hidden. So that's £760 million pounds of taxpayers' money."

"Blimey, that's a hell of a figure."

"Yes, exactly. I need to find out who sets them up? Are any of them connected? How do they find their way into Parliament? Who signs them off? Which department handles the finance? Who gets involved in the civil service? I have a suspicion it may be the same people controlling all the operations? Having squirrelled away such a huge amount of money makes them extremely powerful people. Are you getting the picture, GH?"

"Yes, sir. What immediacy do you want on this?"

"Don't hand this to just anyone. It needs someone who can think outside the box. If this is as big as I think it is, we are in no rush. Take your time to choose an operative, and if I am right, there will be some pretty big cookies involved who will have claws everywhere, nasty claws. Your choice needs to be able to handle themselves and piece it all together on their own. It has no time limit except it needs to be started in my tenancy."

"I'll give it my immediate attention, Prime Minister. It may take some time to choose the correct candidate, and it won't be easy. I'll come back to you when I've chosen the correct person."

"Good, we're done here then, GH, and on this matter, phone me at any time. It's really important to me."

George Henry Smith was the first black man to be selected as the head of MI6, or SIS, as it was now known.

In March 1947, George's father had set off from Jamaica for Great Britain, looking for a new future in his Mother Country. The Ormonde landed in Liverpool, England, which is where most of its black passengers stayed. Harold Smith and his two friends were all qualified and experienced in their own different fields and had been told to use their savings to get to London and find lodgings, which is where they would get work more easily than Liverpool.

Harold Smith, an engineer; Stephen Walford, a fisherman; and John Forder, a carpenter, found digs quite easily south of the river Thames in Worcester Park. One year later, when the HMS *Empire Windrush* landed at Tilbury Docks, London, things became more difficult. These later immigrants did not get the reception they expected and had a great deal of trouble finding decent work.

On 22 June 1948, when the *Windrush* arrived on London Tilbury Docks, "No Irish, no blacks, no dogs" were the all-too-familiar boards stuffed behind the worn curtains of most boarding houses in London and in full view for all to see from the front of the house.

Luckily, Harold and his two friends were ahead of the main rush of Jamaicans and considered themselves British citizens, even though they had experienced the indignity of doors slammed in their faces. By a stroke of luck, by coming straight to London and a year in front of the men from the *Windrush*, they all got employed easily. Stephen Walford took a job as a porter in the Billingsgate Fish Market, where his great strength and knowledge of fish put him above the average and meant he was in popular and secure demand. John Forder took a job as a bin man for the local council. He would often bring furniture home which was damaged that households had thrown out. He repaired the chairs and sofas and was able to make their home more comfortable. Harold himself got employed on the London Underground. They shared a house together which had been bomb-damaged, and it was John who was able to repair items, such as the stove and plumbing and anything which needed welding, and Stephen often brought home from the market the fish which had not sold that day, which gave them a good meal.

Harold had met Chandice at their local church in Jamaica and had been married during the war. She was a nurse and came over to England three years after Harold landed. She couldn't find work as a nurse and took a teacher's assistant job at the local school, as it would fit in with the children better anyway. They moved to a small rented terraced house in Morden, where some other immigrant families had settled and felt fortunate as there had been fewer jobs in Jamaica before she left, even with the qualifications they had.

Two years later, Roy was born, and eighteen months later, James came along. Harold and Chandice wanted James to start school before having more children, and so Danielle was born in 1965, and George Henry was born in 1968. To those in the Smith household, George Henry was pronounced Judge Henry when spoken quickly.

Although they suffered a lot of abuse, like all the Jamaican immigrants, Harold and Chandice tried to understand how people felt. They chose to ignore it and be kind, diligent and industrious. They knew that education was a way out for the children, and although they were not allowed to use their own qualifications to better their position, they knew that a fairly strict regimen for homework and extra study as soon as the children returned from school, they had two hours around the dining room table while being looked over or helped by either Chandice or Harold on his days off. Both children had it drilled into them that exams had to be passed if they wanted any choice in their lives. Harold and Chandice decided to wait until the first two were nearer to getting into big school before having Danielle and George Henry two years later. Harold had managed to gain a promotion dealing with track maintenance which meant he was on permanent nights. Candice and Harold knew that this wasn't ideal, although very soon, he would be working twelve-hour shifts, which gave him three nights on and four days off.

The Beatles had turned the country upside down a few years before, and Carnaby Street thumped to a new musical beat. London was humming. Danielle had been at the top of her class. Henry George was as bright and had the determination and concentration to rival all of his peers. They both excelled to the delight of their parents.

Danielle studied to become a teacher, and Henry George took Economy and Politics at the London School of Economics. He then went on to take a PhD in Psychology at Birkbeck University London.

CHAPTER 26

London Headquarters SIS
Office of the Chief of the Secret Intelligence Service
Mr George Henry Smith BSc, PhD
July 2020

Verity Hawley, their main recruiting officer, raised her voice to make herself heard.

"Boss, computers on this floor are all down."

"Yes, mine's down too, Verity. Check the other floors, please, and report back," he replied.

Sean Willis, who worked in recruitment with Verity, said, "Electricity for the whole building has gone off. Wait a minute looks like the whole street."

George Henry raised his voice.

"Hilary, can you come in, please."

When Henry George had taken over the job of head of MI6, he had argued for an open office. His philosophy was that the more everyone knew, the more efficient and the greatest value was to be had from accumulated intel. His own office was all glass, and he advocated an open-door policy. They all had access to a boardroom that would seat twelve and provided the privacy needed for any matters involving national security, VIPs, and that sort of occasion.

Even before he had finished saying the sentence, Hilary hurried into George Henry's office.

"Sir?"

"Hilary gets everyone armed. I want two on every door, windows stairs up and down. *Now*."

George Henry dialled a number.

"Armoury. We could be under attack. I want all operatives to be given arms and ammo automatic Brownings, pistols, and sniper guns. Must have ID and emergency code to take equipment. It's happening *now*."

George Henry came out of his office like a steam train at full speed, only this apparition was like a male stallion reared up on its hind legs, snorting as it gained a foothold on the floor, bringing its front legs hard down, scattering dust and anything else frightened by its might and rippling muscles. He was at full steam now. He felt more in control as more facts came in, and he had to assess that SIS were not being singled out. He mustn't rule that out until he was sure.

"Andy and Wayne, get the other heads up here fast. We'll meet in five minutes."

He turned pointed at a young man moving between the desks.

"Harry delegate help and find as many candles as possible, torches, batteries, paraffin lamps—anything that can make light and get them in here ten minutes."

"Amanda, would you mind finding ways to feed everyone tonight? I think it's going to be a long one!"

"OK, GH. It will probably mean I have to leave the building." She smoothed her crumpled top down over her more than ample body, proving that to be a language head, you don't need to be superbly fit.

"Yes, and don't go alone. Make sure it's safe, and we'll try to understand what's happened before you do."

"I'll take a headcount straight away."

"Looks like it's the whole city, boss," Tom said as he ran in through the main swing doors. Out of breath, slim and muscled, he cut a fine figure for a young athlete catching his breath and taking deep gulps to bring his breathing quickly back to normal.

"Everything's gone down, GH: computers, landlines, mobiles."

GH replied in a calm voice, "Could be a cyber-attack if it's not localised. You know, in the seventies, we had power cuts and then days when we had no electricity at all for two or three days, and we survived just fine. Don't panic."

George Henry retreated into his office, where his mantra was to never close his door. In this instance, he knew something serious was about to crack off. He laughed at himself as he felt he was about to jump off a cliff into the unknown without a parachute. He needed time to think carefully as the pandemonium reigned outside and answers were needed quickly. He must not make any wrong moves.

One question sprung to mind, which was why the emergency lighting did not come on. Did possibly mean whoever the perpetrators were might already be in the building, controlling the computer?

Andy was the computer guy, and he would back with Wayne soon with all his section heads when they could more clearly bring together the intel and start to make a plan. They started to arrive in his office, which was just big enough to accommodate the seven of them, so they squashed in some on the floor, some in chairs and GH sitting on the desk, which he had pushed against the wall with Sean's help, as he was one of the fit ones. GH and Sean sat on the desk.

GH had to find the solution to his burning question, asking Andy why the computer had not kicked in. Andy was in control of the business section and specialised in computers. He was sweating by this time and was, in his own admission, overweight.

"Well, let's just suppose that whoever set this up was able to produce a virus that could stay dormant in a system for a certain period. In other words, the normal firewalls and antivirus techniques we currently use could not detect the new virus because it was dormant and therefore didn't trigger the responses we had set in place. The main computer goes down after the dormancy period, and it should send a message to start up the standby, but the message is obstructed by the virus which had lain in the cable, and therefore, the message has not reached the standby, and it does not give us the emergency power we need right now. I went straight up to the top floor, where the main hard drives are. Listen to this. They said our satellites have been picking up Russian and Chinese mobile nuclear launching pad movements, and their positions put us in jeopardy—in other words, firing range."

GH looked at Andy. "Do you know how long that has been going on and why we weren't told?"

No one was able to answer, and by this time, the other staff who had been sent on several different missions had come back onto the main office.

"Everything's gone down, boss."

Throughout the whole city, more like."

"No one has any answers."

"OK, everyone, well done. We will collate all the intel you have managed to get after I've had a little chat. I want you all to think for a moment. We are an elite force, and if we had been under physical attack, most of you would be dead."

He let the words sink in for a full minute.

"Those of you who had gone out of the office to get the intel, when you had made it back through those doors, you would have been met with death and destruction, probably with a lead bullet between your own eyes."

He paused a moment.

"I am as much at fault as you are. We all are. We were not prepared for this."

He paused again.

"Only together can we anticipate what goes on inside the head of, say, a terrorist. This is not a bollocking. In fact, you should be bollocking me. It is my responsibility to protect us all. We were not prepared. We had not expected this. Together, collectively, we can work out what has brought this on. It is obviously our main priority. We need to spread our wings and open our thoughts and share every slice of our imaginations. There is a person or persons out there who did this. We know when and what. We want to know how, why and who. What triggered this, the Russian and Chinese nuclear weapon movements? Is it terrorist?"

GH looked across at Andy.

"Is this a computer glitch? Is it contained in this country alone?

Are we being targeted, or is it international? Some landlines are working. They might be on old systems which are less computerised. Otherwise, we need to commandeer vehicles and fuel. We need bedding and food. Our families must be kept informed as to our movements and progress. GCHQ could have intel? Is that enough to keep you busy for the next couple of hours?"

The room exploded with noise.

GH motioned his hands downwards to make his voice heard.

"One more thing: What if we gave ourselves a night at home tomorrow night, which would give us all the opportunity to explain and calm everyone's fears? See how many cars we would need to deliver us home with a morning pick up? Public transport is going to be out of the question."

He had made headings from all the intel collected in the short time they had been together. They made for fascinating reading. All computers and telephone systems in and around their vicinity were non-functional. The city of London had ground to a halt. Transport was not operating. Most landlines were down, but some were working.

GCHQ reported all computers down, except those linked to satellites. They also confirmed the nuclear movements of China and Russia. They also had a story of a hacker gaining entrance to their premises with a connection to 10 Downing, nothing working except the link to the United States. Reports from the US claimed similar computer malfunctions and military connections cut and inoperable. There were rumours that the PM had tried to resign. Also, the deputy PM was injured by the same senior security officer, namely Simon Knight.

MI5, in the same building as SIS, had a similar set of malfunctions. There was a report of a Downing Street senior security officer killing five of their operatives.

Extra information:

All railways, airlines, and airports were not working.

Road transport was working as usual.

"Like me, you must all be thinking, 'What is going on?' Is this the work of a large international group, or could it be a smaller independent group working on their own? Which are we dealing with? What are your thoughts?"

Ideas ebbed and flowed like the tides on a shore, gaining more ground and reaching higher up the beach. Some in the group took one piece of intel and followed it all the way, and others wanted to link two or three paths to get more sense out of the information.

"At this stage, I really don't want to steer your thoughts. I need to talk to the PM. MI5 and GCHQ. So, you all carry on. I'll take Hilary with me and catch up with you all later, and we can all camp here tonight and try to make some sense of it all. Catch you all later."

He caught sight of Hilary and nodded, and they walked towards the exit

CHAPTER 27

Brett Caddick asked his PA to bring GH and Hilary into his office.

"Terrible situation we have on our hands, GH. Have you got any leads?"

"What can you tell me about your security chief, sir?"

"Simon? First-class security chief—intelligent, smart, resourceful, fit, and, to be honest, the best person I have ever dealt with in that position. I know he's missing. Have you got any information about him, GH?"

"That business with Peter Newton, you mean?"

"Yes, we can start there. Why is there more?"

"Well, yes, sir, there are a couple of questions if you don't mind, sir."

"OK, fire away."

"Let's take Peter Newton first."

"Well, they apparently went back to Afghanistan, both in the special services. Peter was an officer, Simon a sergeant who took a party to rescue Peter and saved his life. It didn't end well, because when they met up here in Downing Street, you could tell there was tension between them. Mostly from Peter's side as far, as I could see. Then we had that funny business when Peter had taken Simon to GCHQ and then decided to come back on his own. Somehow, they ended up in a fight somewhere along the A40. Five MI5 agents dead and Peter badly beaten up, and that was the last we have seen of Simon. Then this massive computer crisis worldwide. Still no sign of Simon."

"You had two trips out to the North Atlantic, didn't you, sir? Who did you take with you?"

"Yes, that's right. Took Simon both times."

"What took place on the *George W Bush*, please, sir?"

"Climate change discussions."

"What about climate change, sir?"

"Well, I can't discuss what went on, as it was classified."

"With respect to everything that has gone off this last five days, it would be better if SIS was informed, as I don't want to include in my report that you were unhelpful, sir."

"Yes, of course. I do apologise. Only, some of this information is exceptionally sensitive, GH."

"Let's make it easier for you, sir. Did anything unusual occur before, during, or after the meeting?"

"Meetings, GH. There were two in total. The only thing I can think of is that before the first meeting, MI5 asked to see Simon because they had some new equipment, they wanted him to test, they asked my permission which I gave, and someone saw him here at Number 10."

"There is a rumour you are resigning, sir. Is that true?"

"No, that is not true and seems to have been started by my deputy Peter Newton."

"Thank you, that could be useful. Was there a conclusion to the climate change discussions?"

"There was some talk of trying to dramatically reduce emissions."

"How would you have achieved that, Prime Minister?"

"Yes, well, we couldn't come to an agreement."

"Who was present, sir?"

"Heads of state for Russia, France, Germany, Netherlands, Canada, Australia, New Zealand."

"Ourselves and the States too, sir?"

"Yes, of course, and the president called the meeting. Otherwise, nothing else, except I can remember Simon having a very nice-looking American lady officer escort him around the ship during both the meetings."

His PA knocked and put his head around the door to let him know he was already late for an extraordinary cabinet meeting and they were all waiting. At this point, he excused himself, shook their hands in a hurried manner, and all but fell over himself to get out of the room quickly.

GH and Hilary came out into a smaller office, where a secretary was furiously banging down on the keys of an old-fashioned black Imperial typewriter, so hard and fast that GH was surprised not to see one of the strikers' arms become detached and fly across the room. As they crossed the office onto a large landing, they looked at one another with raised eyebrows, as if to say there was more he wasn't letting on about.

They made their way onto Downing Street and walked off towards SIS headquarters. Back in the main office, the different teams were all starting to return, like them, with all sorts of different bits of intel. GH worked with Hilary and put all the information onto the whiteboard in the main room, where they were gathering to exchange all they had gleaned and allow everyone to access the whole picture.

"OK, first of all, is everyone clear about settling in for the night? Do we have food and bedding?" There was confirmation that they had all they needed for the overnight.

"We'll go through the first reports back that you have on the intel we have up to date," GH said, "and then we can all pick the ones we are best suited to follow up. All agreed?"

Hilary collated all the available information that had been quickly procured. She read off the three boards.

"Brett Caddick needs a visit. Sean, do you want to visit him at Downing Street? We need more info on the meeting if you can get it out of him, which is unlikely. Try to push national security. There seems to be something he is holding back. Get as much off him about the *George W Bush*. Who was there, and what were they there to discuss? Who he mixed with and how long theyb stayed. Anything to prise out more than GHS and I were able to get." The room burst out laughing. GH smiled and shook his head at her, enjoying the joke.

"Next on the list is the deputy PM, Peter Newton. Now we have other information that he was involved in a fight and looked to come off the worst. A few questions spring to mind. Why was he travelling alone at his level of security? Who gave him the bloody nose? Watch this one. He's the snake in the grass. He has a reputation for being sneaky and can be slimy? Overly ambitious. Verity, you look like you would like to tackle our Mr Newton. You OK on your own?"

Verity said, "I've dealt with worse. I'll look out for his dark side."

"This one has come up out of nowhere. They are often the ones who produce the most interesting answers, Professor Paul English, who was Simon Knight's best friend at Cambridge. I can see from the corner of my eye that the boss and I are to take him on.

Anyone who had been in the navy knew this was aimed at Tom Powell. Five feet nine inches and muscled and fit, he was one of the science techs. "Yeah, that's good for me. I still have close contacts and some who are still in the service who are high up now, and I'm stuck here with you lot." Big eruption of laughter and ribald comments to this extremely popular and good-looking team member.

"We know the PM and this Simon Knight spent time on the *George W*, and if you have any contacts that can get through to the aircraft carrier and anything at all that could possibly be useful, thanks, Tom." They all knew Tom was the one she had a bit of a soft spot for, disregarding their nearly twenty-year age gap.

SIS and MI5 were running through a rough patch in their relationship. It hadn't always been so bad, but at that moment over the last few years, they viewed each other's operatives with derision and suspicion, which made each of their sensitive jobs more difficult, and GHS had on his "things to do list" patch-up MI5 and SIS.

Andy Peach was the least likely of any of them to offend the people upstairs in MI5. He was a touch overweight, not tall but easy-going and affable, with a great computer brain. In fact, he was the guy from whom MI5 had sought help in that department in the past.

"You still have friends upstairs, Andy?"

"Well, I don't send them postcards when I'm on holiday, if that's what you mean, but there are a few I can speak to."

"Great, Andy, thanks. So, Wayne, that leaves it to you to take a trip to GCHQ, who will have a stack of intel on nuclear weapon movements, the deputy PM, Simon Knight, and even what the PM himself knows. A little bird tells me a Colonel Grant might be a good starting place there. Hope that's useful, Wayne."

That leaves Auntie Brenda, Amanda. She is the sister of Simon Knight's mother. She is the lady who brought Simon Knight up after his mother committed suicide and his father had taken to alcohol dying shortly after his wife. She still lives where he went to school and is awfully close to him, as you can imagine. She's a retired schoolteacher who seemingly lives a very ordinary life.

GHS regained his feet and said, "Thanks, Hilary. That will give us all a good start to try to tie this monster down and know where to concentrate next. Please remember, we are all on the same team. Don't hold anything back as we work together. We are a very much stronger force working together than on our own. It's better fun too. This Simon Knight character certainly seems to be at the hub of all the trouble and is of great interest."

CHAPTER 28

Paul English had started the day quite normally: he had a bit of banter with the kids concerning the breakfast food they considered enough for a day at school, and he took the dog out for his half hour. He returned, had some toast, showered, and cycled into the Cambridge University computer sciences building.

He sat at a side table in his office and opened up his computer. His door was suddenly opened, and his secretary walked in, followed by two people he had never seen before. The male was black with neatly cropped hair that was greying at the temples, not tall but very wide and athletic looking. His eyes were brown and piercing. The blond young lady with him was a little taller, serious looking, wearing a light grey business suit to the knee and blue shoes with just enough heel to accentuate her slender muscled legs.

"Sorry, Paul, they asked if you were in and came straight through. They wouldn't wait for me to ask if you were free."

"Don't worry, Jane. I've been expecting them."

He turned to the male. "I'm George Henry Smith, head of SIS, and this is Hilary Payne, my assistant, Professor."

"I have been expecting a visit, and here you are. Do sit down."

"Why would you be expecting us, Professor?"

"You know why you're here. Would you like a coffee?"

"Yes, please. We both take black, no sugar."

Paul English remained calm, as though people whom he didn't know barged into his office every day. He picked up his phone and asked Jane to bring the coffee through, please.

"So, I must be in trouble?"

"I wouldn't say that, Professor English. We are not here to cast blame or cart you off to the Tower of London. The more you can help us now, the quicker will we be able to complete a full picture."

"OK, just to make sure we are on the same page, to what exactly are you referring?"

Paul English had been wondering when someone would join the dots and he would get a knock on his door.

"It is conjecture at the moment. A crime may have been carried out, and if it was, we don't know why it was. Would you have any idea as to what I may be referring, Professor?"

At that moment, Jane came in with the coffees. She looked very worried and asked Paul if he was OK.

"Yes, honestly, Jane, it would be better if no one knew about this meeting, please."

"Of course, Paul." She took another worried look at him to make sure he was ok and not under any threat, and left the room.

There followed a very long silence. The sort of silence that sits in a room so all the noises away from that confinement become plainly heard. In the next room, Jane's chair had a squeak, the rolling noise of a file drawer being opened, the rustle of paper, the ping of a computer terminal. As they all knew, the first one to speak had the most to lose. After some time, Professor English looked GHS in the eye and asked, "Is this in connection with my good friend Simon Knight?"

"Yes, it is," said GHS in a friendly well-practised manner.

"OK, well, if I come clean with the information I have, can I be sure it won't get Simon into deep bother."

"I hate to say this to you, but I can't honestly give you that confirmation without knowing the full facts. To be really honest, at the moment, it looks as if the pair of you are in it right up to your eyeballs."

"Yes, I figured you would say that. In for a penny, in for a pound. About three months ago Simon phoned me and said he was in a dilemma and needed help, and could he come and see me in private?

I chose here and after office hours. He had been summoned to accompany the PM on a mission to meet the US president, the precis of which was that US scientists had confirmed knowledge that the earth had a massive climate calamity brewing, which meant that within six months, the temperature would have risen a whole degree. Three months later, it would have risen a further one and a half degrees and would rise exponentially thereafter. Within the year, life on earth as we know it would have ceased to exist."

"Bloody hell, Professor. How the hell did he come by this information?"

"He was there to check the security before the Prime Minister arrived."

"Slow down, Professor. There's an awful lot of information which is difficult to take in all in one bite. Are you saying the meeting was on an American aircraft carrier which was moored here in the UK?"

"No, the USS *George W Bush* was moored somewhere south of Iceland in the North Atlantic. He was flown out on a fighter jet."

"This is starting to go beyond the bounds of believability, Professor." GHS looked across at Hilary, who gave him a shrug of her slender shoulders as if to say, *We may as well hear it all.*

"Carry on then, Professor."

"I know you have found this first part of the story unbelievable; I have to warn you, the next bit gets even worse."

"Who was there?"

"The US, UK, Canada, Germany, Russia, France, Holland, Australia and New Zealand."

"Go on."

"Ethan Miller introduced two scientists who went through the scientific data thoroughly and gave them all the facts the US scientists had collated. Ethan Miller asked the scientists to go back to their cabins. He then said that the main perpetrators were China, North Korea, India, and other Southern Hemisphere countries' manufacturing, mainly and using coal as their preferred choice of power. He then outlined polluting the atmosphere from overpopulation as well. He insisted they had no time to come to any sort of unilateral agreement in the time frame to make any difference and that if they reacted immediately, it was the only way they could possibly save the planet. He didn't know what the actual course of action was to take but that something had to be done and it had to be done straight away. He explained that is why he called everyone together. It all had to be secret, or if it got out, there could be rioting on the streets if people thought they had only six months to live."

"You are right. It just got worse. That was it? I can't digest this. What did they all say?"

"Complete mayhem. They took over half an hour to calm down.

"So, how did Simon Knight get hold of this information?"

"I'm not quite sure, Mr Smith."

"Christ almighty, Professor."

In all the years she had worked for him, Hilary had never heard GHS blaspheme in her presence before. If he had asked her what she thought, she would have said the Professor was telling the truth. It was an extraordinary story, but it wasn't far away from what most educated people believed was eventually going to happen anyway, except that this climate calamity was not expected for another few hundred years.

"Simon was put in a complete dilemma. Who could he trust with this information, and then, what could he do anyway? He knew he couldn't trust either MI5 or SIS, as he knew no one at either. They might even decide to eliminate him, possibly the only safe conclusion considering the knowledge he had stumbled onto. He even thought about coming clean with the PM but decided that might lead to all sorts of avenues he could not control. So, he told me—we are old pals—and that's how he ended up at my door."

Hilary asked Paul English how he himself had reacted.

"Like you, I found the story incredible, completely incredible. I needed to think the whole thing over, and we met a week later. That's really when the position we were in became even worse."

GHS leaned forward and said, "Think I'm ahead of you here, Paul. You're going to tell us that Ethan Miller had the whole thing mapped out from the beginning?"

"You know then, do you, Mr Smith? You know about the second meeting and developing the nuclear bombing strategy of foreign territory?"

"What the fuck are talking about? Sorry, Hilary, but this is getting horribly unreal. What second meeting, Paul? You have only just mentioned the bombshell in the first meeting."

Paul didn't want him to know that at the first meeting, Miller had suggested the use of military force, and at the second, he got them to agree to nuclear deterrents.

"The second meeting on the *George W Bush* aircraft carrier."

George Henry rolled forward and, with his elbows on his knees, allowed his head to flop down onto his cupped hands. He shook his head in total incredulity.

"Paul tell me you are joking. Tell me this isn't true, please."

"Let me tell you: our reaction was just the same."

George Henry sat up straight, looked at Paul English who said, "As we hold each other by the balls, so to speak, I am telling you all I know: it's the truth."

"Hold on steady, Paul. Can I ask why Russia was not at the second meeting? Am I right? Am I right about that? They were not at the second meeting?"

"That's right," answered Paul English. "How the hell did you know?"

"They switched sides after the first meeting and went with the Chinese—that's why. It makes complete sense now. I already knew Russia and China were up to something strange together."

"So that's why they were not at the second meeting, crafty buggers. Always out to hurt the West."

"Walk a mile in the other guy's shoes, Paul. We were potentially out to hurt the East."

"That's true. That is probably why they don't trust any of us anymore. I feel I must come clean. At the first meeting, Miller, along with the earth ending, suggested they all use normal military weapons."

"While I think about it, Paul, how come you were able to listen to the second meeting. Did you and Simon come up with a little scheme?"

"To be honest, yes, Simon brought it straight back here because MI5 did not have a fix when exactly Simon would get back in the F-35. I had set up a computer to break the code. He wanted my evaluation about what was cracking off. So we listened together this time. It allowed me to verify that everything Simon had told me was true."

"How did you manage the technicalities to achieve that, Paul?"

"You must remember that the students who leave here have taken all their knowledge from me. I, however, have not given all my knowledge to them, and from that gap, I was able to set up a computer that could read the silicon listening device. Simple, Dr Watson."

They all laughed, which was able to break the tension which had gradually been building up over the last hour. There was a knock, and Jane put her head round the door and said she had heard the laughter and thought it safe to ask if anyone needed anything.

"Good timing, Jane. Perhaps you could show Hilary our facilities, and George Henry can come with me."

They all returned several minutes later with refreshed mugs of tea and looking very much relieved.

The two men nodded at one another, showing mutual respect. Paul English wondered whether he might be hauled off in handcuffs at the end and if he had been too open. He thought Simon would have agreed with his tactics.

Paul English taken the decision at the start to tell the whole truth and still wasn't quite sure it had been the correct one.

George Henry, on the other hand, had been taken aback by this earnestly honest professor who had, he and Hilary silently agreed, taken the bull by the horns at whatever cost. It certainly gave him plenty to work on and tied in most of the intel his department had been able to piece together.

"What happened next then, Paul?"

"On the second tape, Ethan Miller said the only potion was to use nuclear."

"What? Are you telling me that the American president suggested using nuclear power?"

"That is correct. As unbelievable as it seems. I listened to the tape myself."

George Henry asked "What happened next Paul?"

"Well we decided that we might be able to design a virulent virus which, through the channels at Simons disposal at Number 10, could be administered into military establishments primarily to stop the nuclear detonations and any telecommunications—also to infiltrate manufacturing and airlines and trade in order to slow pollution. The idea was to have a virus that would get into a system and lie low, thus making it undetectable because it wasn't active, and antivirus programmes wouldn't know it was there. That part of it was my job. Simon's job was to dispatch it to as many facilities as possible. I have to say, we didn't realise it was as strong and virulent as it was. It surpassed all our expectations."

"At great expense worldwide, Paul."

"What would have been the cost if we hadn't reacted the way we did, George Henry?"

"I can't answer that today. Let's cut to the chase. Where will I find Simon Knight?"

"I knew you would ask me that. There is only one answer."

"Which is?"

"I honestly don't know where Simon is. He said he would disappear. As I told you, he's a smart cookie and will take some finding. I really don't know. We discussed this, he and I, and we concluded this was the best way. He won't have told anyone."

"Who else knew you were designing this virus? Why didn't you go to a higher authority?"

"Don't think we didn't discuss that as well. We already knew the highest person was our own prime minister. We already knew he had already agreed to follow the nuclear plan. We didn't trust the police. The higher we looked, the less we could trust them. The services follow the Crown, who follow the government. We didn't really know anyone to trust in MI5 or SIS, so we decided to follow our instinct and keep it 'in house', so to speak. What will happen to me now Henry George?"

"All this has to be decided at a higher level, Paul."

"Do you think we might get long sentences? I have been worried about the government's reaction."

"To be honest, I do need to verify as much of what you have told me and then need to think some. My initial reaction could be that the fewer people outside SIS who know about this, the better. I need to talk it through with the other members of my department."

CHAPTER 29

Graham Bennett, Foreign Secretary, sat at his mahogany desk, his elbows resting on the red leather writing surface inlaid with a gold leaf pattern around the edges. His direct phone line rang, he picked it up.

"Hello, it's George Henry Smith, sir."

"Hello, GH, how are you?"

"I'm fine. Thank you, sir. I've got some disturbing news that's just come to my attention."

"Go ahead, GH."

"This intel is top secret. Only the PM knows, and he doesn't know I'm phoning you. MI5 know about it too."

"Wait, GH. This sounds out of order to me."

"Let me tell you, and then you can judge."

"OK, go ahead. I hope I can trust you."

"Thank you. Two weeks ago, the American president called a meeting with most Western heads of state on the USS *George W Bush* aircraft carrier, which was moored south of Iceland. At the meeting, he dropped the bombshell: he had scientific evidence that due to pollution from manufacturing and overpopulation, the figures for climate change had become exponential, and the earth was heating up at an extremely fast rate. His evidence suggested that within six months, the temperature on earth would rise by five degrees and all human life would not be able to survive."

"Bloody hell, GH, are you sure of your facts?"

"Yes, I'm afraid I am, sir. It gets worse. His solution is to use nuclear weapons to obliterate most of the Far East, including China, Africa, India, and North Korea. There was a second meeting in which all the nations agreed unilaterally to comply with his solution."

"So, that accounts for the Russian and Chinese mobile launchpad movements picked up by GCHQ?"

"That is what it looks like. Russia was invited to the first meeting and didn't attend the second."

"OK, so those two have joined forces to obstruct his intention."

"Looks like it."

"Where are you at with this at the moment?"

"I'm having the evidence unearthed, and then the sources checked over. I would suggest the fewer people who knew about this, the better."

"Definitely, I agree. What do you want me to do?"

"Give me twelve hours, and I can come back with news on the sources."

"I know William Hassop-Greene at MI5. I'll see what gives there till tomorrow first thing then."

The two men each put their phones down and took a deep intake of breath. Life rarely threw such a crooked ball at you.

William Hassop-Greene's phone went, he picked it up.

"Sir, the foreign secretary's here to see you. He's on his way in."

"William, how are you?" His piercing green eyes looked straight at the head of MI5 as William Hassop-Greene ran his fingers through his wavy brown hair, which was a shade too long and needed putting back in place as it flopped over his young-looking fresh face. His tall stature meant he was eye to eye with Hassop-Greene.

"Surprised Graham, have we dispensed with the normal pleasantries of making appointments?"

"I don't have time to be pleasant, William. I have been sitting on this for four years and have waited to see if you have any honour about you at all. The answer is that you haven't."

"What do you mean? You can take that back. How dare you?"

"I have had you under surveillance for a number of years. Shady rumours here, a bad smell there. You seem to extract yourself from the mire and come out smelling clean. This time, I am not going to hold back. The account is in the name of your wife Sonia Hassop-Greene, number 26784479, sort code 60-45-88 Lloyds Bank, Guernsey, £12,500,000. It has sat there gaining interest for three years and four months. Who else has access to this account, William? You do. Where did it come from? Climate Change Development. You managed, through your dirty web of politicians and civil servants, to tuck it away, never to be seen again."

William Hassop-Greene had gone completely white. In fact, this whole head was dappled with red blotches on a white and sweaty background. He was wiping away the streams of perspiration as though he had run a marathon and then sat in a sauna. Graham Bennett knew he had too many facts that were completely correct for Hassop-Greene to argue with.

"What do you want, you bastard?"

"You have one chance to get his right. If you don't tell me all, you know you will be taken straight down the Nick and won't see the light of day for years. If you don't believe me, ring your PA and ask her how many policemen there are waiting outside your office."

Hassop-Greene, never taking his eyes off the foreign secretary, picked his phone up and pressed a switch.

"Shirley, is the foreign secretary accompanied by anyone, dear?"

"Five," he shouted down the phone.

"What happens if I comply?"

"You will get home tonight, which will enable you to return your cut and get the rest of the £26 million from your nasty little gang and get it in a parliamentary account. I may then stand up for you in court, and you may get a smaller custodial sentence. Tell me everything you know about the two meetings in the North Atlantic. I need to know every detail of the climate change calamity the US president outlined and the countries who signed up to the nuclear-weapon solution."

William Hassop-Greene had to hold onto his desk to stop himself from falling from his chair onto the floor.

Forty-five minutes later, Graham Bennett had the information he wanted on his mobile.

"That is all, William?"

Hassop-Greene nodded, unable to speak any more.

George Henry spoke into his mobile "You can come in, Inspector."

"Wait a moment. You said I would get home tonight."

"I realised in the end that I really couldn't trust you."

He waited until William Hassop-Greene had been cautioned, manacled and led away. He spoke into his mobile again."

"Fraud? I've got a big one for you." Half an hour later, he was on the phone again to the foreign secretary of the United States of America.

"Frank? It's Graham. We have a problem. Let me tell you a story about your president, Ethan Miller."

"Hey, Graham, as I've told you before, there are plenty of people over this side of the pond who would like to see him finished. He's not really trustworthy."

"Well, this may be an impeachment."

"You go ahead, buddy. I'm all ears.

CHAPTER 30

Darkly and Jane left the hotel and set off west away from Pennsylvania, heading for Montana. When he landed in the US, he had bought a used Ford Ranger Raptor 2.5-litre auto pick up with a tow bar. He had planned to drive at a steady sixty-five miles an hour, which wouldn't attract any state police attention. They would drive for fifteen hours and find a motel for the night. The distance was important, as he knew he would be hunted down like a wanted criminal. A good start was essential. When they came after him, he wanted the trail to be as cold as possible if he was going to successfully hide away and not alert anyone's attention.

They were soon out of Pennsylvania, leaving Lake Erie and on past Detroit and heading for Ohio.

Jane asked, "Why are you buying extra fuel cans every time we stop for fuel? Wouldn't it be quicker to just fill up the tank every time we stop?"

"Yeah, it would. Before we arrive at the end of our journey the pumps at petrol stations may not be working and also it means that towards the end of the journey we won't be stopping at service stations and won't be drawing attention to ourselves also it means I can build up my reserve of fuel cans for my outboard motor."

"Outboard motor, Darkly?"

"Yeah, for my inflatable."

"Inflatable?"

"How else do you think I will be able to fish and be self-sufficient. I think I need to explain more to you. To escape England, in self-defence, I killed three or four guys who were trying to kill me. I don't really know why they were trying to kill me, but someone had set them up. Someone, and I think I know who it might be had told them a story about me that was untrue." He looked across at Jane and realised she was shocked and frightened.

"It will probably be SIS who will come looking for me. They are a bit like your FBI. They won't find me straight away because of all these precautions I am taking. The less you actually know, the better. If you don't know where I am, you have done nothing wrong, the safer you will be."

"Darkly, I think it best if you don't meet my parents. I don't want to put them in any danger."

"That's fine, but there is one thing I need you to do for me."

"I'm not going to kill anyone for you, Darkly."

They both laughed, and Jane went on, "Honestly, it does scare me, though. And then there's you. Will you stay safe? Forget the fact that I'm falling in love with an international criminal."

"I've got two other phones. I will have one, although it can't be traced to me, and the other one I want you to have, as an emergency method of getting in touch should anything happen.

"Like what exactly, Darkly?"

"Like the British secret service trying to find me."

"Grief, Darkly, it's a bit dramatic. Sort of FBI stuff, isn't it?"

"It's simple, really. Neither phone has any connection to either of us. If you need me, phone or text, and I can tell you where to find me. The number is programmed in the memory."

"How will you contact me?"

"If I phone you, my cover will have been blown, and I'll be on the move anyway."

"Oh, Darkly, it seems such a bizarre sort of hopeless mess, really. Will this have to go on for long?"

"As long as it takes, I'm afraid." He leaned across and gave her a kiss on the cheek.

As they had talked, they had driven through Ohio, which was a smaller state, and ended up in Indiana, headed for Indianapolis, where they decided to spend the night, as it was going to be busier and nearly impossible to be remembered.

Darkly had also been using his American accent all the time, and Jane had been correcting his pronunciation and when they pulled off the main drag and picked an ordinary motel. Darkly did all the talking quite confidently in a Montana accent. No one back home would know he was travelling with an American passport under the name of Danny Chandler. They parked the pickup securely outside their cabin, went out to get a takeaway meal, and ate in the room.

As they lay on the bed relaxing after their long journey. Darkly leaned over and lifted Jane's hair gently from the side of her neck. Jane responded by kissing him on the side of his temple, put her arm around his back and stroked him, and started to undo his shirt buttons. He held the side of her face in his hand, moving his lips up her neck to her cheek and onto her temple. Jane moaned and pulled away from him a little, sliding her top over her head, removing her bra, and lying back on the bed, taking his head to her breast so he could take her nipple in his lips and massage the beautiful pink bud with his tongue.

Jane finished undoing the buttons on his shirt and pulled it off his muscled torso. She ran her fingers over the tight configuration of Darkly's strong, honed body. She felt an extraordinarily strong urge to have him inside her. She brought her pelvis to his and ground it into his body. Darkly slid his hand down her slim back, down towards her undulating buttocks, and found the base of her spine. He followed it further down and round. Jane undid the button on the front of her jeans and eased them lower to allow his fingers to find her moist womanhood. He caressed her lips until they were very wet and her hips were grinding into him. Jane's whole body arched in a curve, and he looked into her light blue eyes and told her he loved her. Jane undid his trouser button and tugged them down. As he was doing the same to her jeans, he saw that she was not wearing any pants, which he found so sexy, the thought made his manhood even harder. As Jane took his pants off, his piece stood so erect, it gave her the mental vision of her own Adonis. Jane took hold of his erection and guided it into her.

Darkly's experience with women was reasonably limited, but with Jane, he was able to relax sexually when he was making love. He allowed his body to flow with the motion and let himself go without embarrassment or feeling, which meant that curling his lower body to gain deeper penetration came as a totally natural way for them to be taken to a higher level of emotion, giving each of them a higher feeling of belonging to the other.

They both enjoyed a slow rhythm, often playing the ring at the end of his penis over her clitoris until instinctively they knew that this was the time for him to go deeper into her so that Jane could feel his penis far inside her. To conserve the wonderful combination of emotions, they had to enjoy the length of it as it travelled along her sensual glands. Meanwhile, he either dipped his head to take one of her nipples between his lips, which made her arch even more towards his hard erection, or kissed her on her pursed lips and explored the end of her tongue with his as they flicked them together in a dance of erotic joy.

They sensed the eventual eruption when their bodies fused, and he ejected his love into her. Jane gasped air into her hungry lungs as her uncontrolled pelvic movements ground into his.

CHAPTER 31

The following morning, they checked out and headed north-west into Illinois, keeping well south of Lake Michigan and Chicago and enjoying rolling hills and farmland, interspersed with forests and prairies. Darkly had never seen open spaces like these before. The land literally stretched for miles and miles, an eye-opener for him at least. They crossed the Great River Mississippi and into Iowa, more rolling hills and cornfields that stretched as far as the eye could see. They then headed north to Sioux Falls and west again, heading for Chamberlain and the famous bridge over the Missouri River, built originally in 1925—another wide expanse of water using cast iron and many arches pinned together to broach the wide river. Jane explained as much as she knew to Darkly as they travelled, both aware they were soon to part and that they were looking at an uncertain future.

Darkly, on the other hand, explained to Jane the true sequence of events that had led up to the present day. Jane already knew the vital information that he should not have known—and that it might have been this information that indicated the only way for them to be sure he didn't publicise that the story was to kill him. He explained the car chase and how MI5 was trying to do just that.

They climbed up and up as they entered Black Hills National Park. The road through Wyoming kept on high ground, and they knew they were in the Rocky Mountains. The road went downhill into the valley, and they passed Billings Airport, where Jane would eventually catch a flight back to her unit before the road climbed up again over the Belt Mountains before dropping down to Wolf Creek Canyon and Helena, which is where Jane's parents lived.

As they reached the base of the valley, there was a garage where several boats were on sale. Darkly pulled in and parked. This was a good opportunity to get some of the equipment he needed.

A middle-aged man, shorter than Darkly, came over and asked, "Are you looking for anything special, or are you just browsing? My name is Gary. It's my garage."

"No, Gary, I'm not browsing. I do need a few things, but I'm on a tight budget."

"You from around here then?"

"Yes, shall I tell you what I need?"

Darkly outlined the items he had on his list. Gary swept his dark hair off his face and pointed to a twenty-four-foot semi-rigid over to the side of the plot.

"Now we don't get much use for a boat like this one round here. Only, I got stuck with it last year and would be willing to offer a good deal on that. Most people only want something for the lakes. I'll be glad to get rid of it, to be honest."

Darkly wondered: Was Gary setting him up, or was he genuine? He figured to go along with him and see what he would offer, as he needed a seagoing vessel, but he didn't want him to know he was heading for the east coast of Oregon.

In the next forty-five minutes, Darkly had bought himself the twenty-four-foot semi-rigid, a seventy-horsepower outboard, as well as trailer, fishing tackle, lines, buoys, a sleeping bag, a used wetsuit, mask, snorkel and flippers, and the boat had a couple of lobster pots and two square containers under the tonneau cover. The lobsters would go in these to keep them fresh when it was filled with seawater, which Gary threw in for free. He also bought a fishing rod and the appropriate tackle. He bought petrol cans and oil and extra cans of diesel and filled the pickup's tanks. Darkly kept quiet about the four-cylinder diesel engine, which was already on the boat. It was a specialised seagoing engine, adapted for offshore work, but perhaps Gary didn't know what it was worth, as he was used to selling smaller engines more suited for lake use. Darkly knew this engine would give him all the power he would need on the open sea.

They set off with the semi-rigid in tow towards Helena. They had agreed to stop a street short of Jane's parents' house and for Darkly to drive off without any contact. This gave Jane the peace of mind that her parents would learn little to nothing about Darkly, which she thought would be safest.

Darkly pulled up a street away from Marjorie and David Foster's house. He turned towards Jane and said, "Jane, I'm really sorry." Jane leaned forward and put her forefinger on Darkly's lips, and when she removed it, she kissed him tenderly.

"No need to apologise. It is what it is, Darkly. I've fallen in love with an international killer who is on the run from the British secret services. I don't know where or when I will see him again. Has he saved the world from a nasty mistake, or will he be in gaol for a very long time? I know not. What I do know is that I can't stop loving him and will be there when it's all finished. OK?"

Before Darkly could reply, Jane had lugged her holdall from beside her feet, opened the door, and was already on the footpath, waving goodbye to him.

Darkly watched her disappear around the corner and could not help the wretched tugging feeling in his stomach at the thought of their separation. He had to hand it to her: no tricky goodbyes or tongue-tied moments with Jane. One moment, she was telling him how much she loved him, and the next, she was gone.

CHAPTER 32

He checked all around the pickup and trailer. All safe—Tyres good, brakes not heating up on the trailer—so he jumped in and set off. He had to get back up to the top of the range, which he took slowly, taking a circular route back south, leaving Montana and entering Idaho, finally swinging round to the right on the Snake River Plain to miss the worst of the mountain range before heading north-east towards Portland.

It was getting dark by this time, and he had bought food when at the garage, so he chose a pull-in well away from the road and stopped for the night. He slept in his new sleeping bag across the back seat of the pickup. He rose with the sun and felt very hungry, knowing he had to get settled before the end of the day. He came down off the Owyheeite Mountain into the Columbia Plateau and stayed on the valley floor for miles. Darkly found a motel in the middle of nowhere, where he had food and coffee and freshened up. He was starting to feel part of the place with his newly perfected Montana accent. He carried on towards Portland until he turned south again and drove up into Mount Jefferson to reach a camp he had previously chosen. He had booked a cabin here, and he would make this his base.

He found the Sharpman Camp easily. The site was well signed, and once past the notice, the gravel drive led in between two mature trees. Lines of cabins stretched for about fifty yards, then swept to the right, towards the distant woods. In front of him was the site office, and behind that was a shower and toilet block. He parked and entered.

The owner was a short man with a dark complexion and a ready smile. It looked like he ate too well.

"Don't' get many campers at this time of year, Mr Chandler," he said. "Larry Swart's my name. Bought it off Sharpman a few years ago and kept his name."

"Yes, I booked online. I don't really know how long I'll stay, but I'll pay for six months upfront and take it from there, Larry."

"That's great, Danny. That's my special winter price I gave you. You from Montana?"

"Helena. I got the money here."

Darkly handed him the money.

"You can keep the trailer beside the cabin on the grass. You've got a log burner in number sixteen, and you can pick up dead wood out of the forest up the track there." He said, pointing up a dirt lane leading into the woods, which stretched as far as the eye could see. "You can take the pickup. Electricity's from a generator. I turn it on at six, and it runs till ten, when I turn it off. Price is in with the rent. Shower and toilets come at that price too. You'll find it good and quiet at this time of year."

"Thanks, Robert. I'll take the trailer down to Astoria in the morning but leave it here otherwise. Is that OK?"

"Yeah, that's fine. You'll find it cheaper that way." He gave a little laugh and tossed Darkly the keys.

"You've got yourself a good little secluded spot down this line, over to the right. Sixteen's the one on end."

Darkly drove up and expertly backed the trailer onto the grass to the left of the wooden cabin. He left it attached, as he wanted an early start in the morning.

It was indeed in a far corner of the camp, isolated and right up against the trees on two sides, which was where the forest started that Gary had told him about.

He unlocked the solid door and stepped in. It was clean and basic, a lot better than the Royal Navy barracks he was used to. Opposite the front door, the three-quarter bed was on a mezzanine, with a little window looking into the trees. It was above the log burner, which provided heating and the only means of cooking. To one side, there was a small toilet cubicle. All ideal, especially as the last occupant left a few logs in the wicker basket to the other side of the burner. There was one cold-water tap with a basin on a table beneath a window overlooking the woods to the side and a couple of armchairs, each with a wool blanket hung over the back to the left-hand side of the log burner.

It was starting to get late, and Darkly was exhausted. He ate the food he had bought at the garage and took himself up to get some shut-eye. He was exhausted but happy with the way things had fallen into place. He climbed the open wooden steps up to the bed took off his clothes. The minute he crawled under the duvet and rested his head on the pillow, he was asleep.

He woke to the sound of bird song as the dawn heralded the sun rising in the east. No bears or coyotes near, he mused as he listened to the wonderful chorus. The night before, he had noticed under the table a bucket with a jug in it. He took the soap and sports towel from his kit bag, which he had slung onto one of the armchairs. He filled the bucket from the tap, put the jug into the cold water, and went outside and round the cabin and stepped onto the small raised wooden ledge at the gable end overlooking the woods. There were two hooks on the gable end of the cabin. He hung his towel on one hook and quickly stripped off and hung his clothes on the other. He placed one foot in the bucket, took a jugful of water, and slowly emptied it over his head, gasping as he did so. He took the soap and lathered his hair first, then the rest of his body. He filled the jug again and emptied it over his head. The idea of keeping one foot in the water bucket was that all the water he poured onto his head mostly drained back into the bucket, allowing him to have enough water to repeat the process until he was satisfied. He had removed all the suds from his hair, between his legs, and under his arms. He tipped the rest of the water over his upturned face, stepped away from the bucket, and dried himself down, wrapped himself with the towel, took his clothes off the hook, and went back inside the cabin. He got himself as dry as he could and dressed in fresh clothes, brushed his teeth, and hung the towel on the bar inside the front door. He lobbed the clothes in which he had travelled into the bucket, filled it up with water, and dropped some liquid soap in to soak. He had decided to grow a beard. It could disguise him as well as be easier to maintain. He came out, locked the cabin, and got into the pickup and started the engine.

It took him a couple of hours to reach Astoria and head straight for the harbour master's office. He paid his harbour fees and registered his lobster pots. The harbourmaster, Jeff Pitman, wasn't there, so it was his female assistant, Sally, who gave him charts of the area and where to avoid the professional fishermen's preferred fishing sites and where to enter the water.

Darkly drove down to badge holder's car park and backed up the slipway, making sure the pickup had the brakes on before he went around, undoing the straps from the boat onto the trailer. He had a surprise when he realised the trailer had an extra subframe, which extended beyond the normal trailer. It meant that the rear wheels of the trailer did not have to be fully submerged before the boat was able to float, another little extra Gary didn't know about. It would also help If he had to launch off a sandy beach or muddy area because the trailer wheels had less chance to get stuck in the mud or sand. Darkly was sure Gary had not known about this additional feature, or he would have tried to charge more.

Once afloat, he took the painter, led the semi-rigid to the edge of the slipway, and tied it off with two round turns and two half-turns through a ring at the water's edge. He parked the pickup and trailer and walked over to the slipway and boarded the semi-rigid. I took the rest of the tonneau cover off, cantilevered the engine into the water and locked it, and attached the steering wires and throttle connector. He put on his buoyancy aid, jumped off and undid the painter, and this time looped it through the ring on the jetty, keeping hold of the free end. He temporarily tied off the painter on the boat and started the engine. He checked the water jet coming out of the engine to ensure the cooling mechanism was functioning, checked around, put the gear lever into reverse, let the painter go, and dropped the free rope onto the floor and made sure it was all out of the water. He swung the wheel to the left and put the gear lever into the forward position, cleared the jetty, and headed out, remembering the regulation for slow speeds in US ports, which equated to about seven miles an hour. There was a force four forecast rising to force five in two hours, which meant that while he was protected within the estuary from the land on either side, the swell was fairly light, but as soon as he was over the bar, the sea became quite choppy.

He had inflated the sides of the boat to the recommended PSI at the garage and had checked they had kept their charge before launching off the jetty. This gave the boat the rigidity it needed for these sea conditions. As he opened the throttle, the familiar smell of the sea, the taste of the salt, and the wind in his face took him back to his time with the SBS—his years of service, the fun and camaraderie, and the excitement of the work they achieved. All his old comrades missed it when they left, as he did, but there had to be a time to leave, when his body could not cope with the rigours of duty needed to be a safe member of the team.

The boat responded well to the conditions. Darkly was delighted with it and opened up to about three-quarters power, which, in these seas, gave him about eighteen knots. The wind was coming at him over the port bow, with plenty of sprays, and he made good headway. The craft really behaved very well, responsive and light to steer. He had also noted that the propeller was slightly larger than normal, which made a huge difference, especially in seas like this, where the power from the engine and the larger propeller provided exceptional performance. He followed the chart, where he had marked the areas from Sally at the harbour masters office. In about seven fathoms, he dropped anchor and let the boat come round into the wind. He had already set up his rod and cast over the side for bass.

Fifteen minutes later, he had landed three good-sized sea bass. He cut one in half and loaded his lobster pots with half each. He held on to the other two for his tea when he got back. He started the engine, checked the jet, headed for his chosen locations for the pots, marked and dated the chart, gave them each enough line to allow for the tide at that time in the month, and dropped the pots. He checked that the lines weren't pulling on either of the buoys and headed back.

The wind had picked up and was coming up to force five, which was making the sea choppy enough to remain at half throttle, keeping away from the professional fishermen's patch. He would have to wait before giving the boat a speed trial. Today was about getting back safely and in one piece. He made it back to the harbour and along to the jetty and pulled up alongside the slipway.

Darkly found that the extra subframe made it easier to hand winch the boat up onto the trailer, and it wasn't long before all was secured and he was able to prk the trailer in a quiet corner. He called for groceries on his way back and found there was no light or telephone in the shop. This, he knew, was his doing. They were offering huge discounts on all frozen products, but as he had no access to a freezer, so he couldn't buy anything and take advantage of the prices. At the same time, he wondered what huge catastrophe would have resulted had their president gotten away with his plans.

Back at the campsite, Darkly parked up, and took the groceries into the cabin. He took the large wood saw, which he noticed behind the log burner, and put it in the pickup.

He drove the pickup through the trees straight along the track. It was unmade. The surface was mud and shingle, quite rutted through misuse but also straight, with no sharp corners. In the early nineteenth century, Astoria, was named after a New Yorker, John Astor. He had started a fur trade business which was the first American settlement west of the Rockies, . The timber trade came along later, and they had to make the roads straight to get the long tree trunks through the forest and down to the port. Darkly had come across this information when he had been planning where to hunker down and stay out of sight.

He took the pickup along the track for about a mile and pulled into the first clearing on his right. The ground was littered with branches of different sizes, most of it having been there some time. He set about selecting the ones he wanted and used a stump to saw it into a size to fit in the log burner. He filled the back and took the load back to the cabin. There was a recessed area on the side of the cabin next to where he had parked, where he could stack the logs to keep them dry. He filled the recess up to the slanting roof, took the rest inside, and started to light the fire. To the left of the firebox, there was a small oven with a door. He took the bass outside, took out his knife, and slit the front of each fish, throwing the entrails over the fence. He took them inside, washed them and wrapped them in foil, tossed it into the oven, and closed the door. He took a pan of water and placed it on the top of the burner, cut up a couple of unpeeled potatoes, waited until the water boiled, and dropped them into the pan. Five minutes later, he cut the broccoli and put the stems in too. A few more minutes later, he mashed up the potatoes with a bit of butter and served himself. Darkly sat in one of the armchairs, realising the design wasn't for comfort, or maybe they were too old, but the food was delicious.

The following day, Darkly wanted to see if his lobster pots had caught any prey. After making sure everything was in place, he set off for Astoria.

He entered the park and headed towards the trailer. A man, who he took to be the harbourmaster was making his way towards him.

"Danny Chandler?"

"Yes, that's me."

"Hi, Danny. I'm Jeff Pitman. I wasn't in the other day," he said, putting out his hand. Darkly shook it and smiled.

"If we were in season, I probably wouldn't remember your name. This time of year, with not much going on, it's different. You staying local, Danny?"

"Not really. Up in the hills."

"Good craft you have here. Just right for the conditions we get. At the moment, I only have flat-bottom fibreglass, and it's OK within the estuary but no good beyond the bar if the wind's up. A strong wind would flip it over. Oh yes, the reason I wanted to have a word."

Darkly's stomach dropped. *Have they caught up with me already? Are the FBI on my tail? Have I made a mistake?*

Jeff carried on, "At this time of year, we get so little trade, but as I say, I like to see a few boats around, and if you wanted to keep yours here, there would be no charge. Have to change around April, when the season starts, I'm afraid."

"That would be easier for me. Thanks, Jeff."

"No trouble, Danny. Anything you want, drop in and see me, OK?"

"That's kind. Sure will."

They waved, and Jeff sauntered away back to the boat he was inspecting. Darkly thought that if the world had more people like Jeff, it would be a better place to live in. He was settling in to do all the things he enjoyed the most. He launched the semi-rigid and backed away from the slipway.

He waved again to Jeff, who nodded at the craft, and Darkly maintained the correct speed, which gave him the time to enjoy the picturesque view of the houses built on the hills coming down to the sea. The boats bobbed on their moorings, and the dark green kelp, and other seaweed growing below gave plenty of cover to all the species of smaller fish and molluscs and octopus he knew would be on the seafloor. The wind was from the same direction today as before and at a much steadier steady force three. He didn't start opening the throttle until he was clear of the bar.

The sea was flatter than yesterday and allowed him to open up a bit more. The powerful engine took up the speed really well, lifting the boat's body out of the water. This design would never be able to plane, but it did rise up, and the nose lifted a bit, and she flew. Taking each wave in its stride, she ploughed through with great purpose, very steady. This was a great joy for Darkly, who hadn't done much of this for the last ten years since leaving the SBS.

He was up to his lobster pots in no time. He throttled back and came into the wind, dropped anchor, and allowed the boat to take hold on the seabed. He tied the anchor rope off and turned off the engine. The lapping of the water accompanied him as he put a square blue flag on the bow of the boat, stripped off, pulled on his wetsuit and flippers, put his weight belt on, and spat in his mask. He washed it out, splashed his face, made sure his knife was in place, positioned the mask over his face, put his snorkel in his mouth, and backflipped over the side of the boat. He snorkelled over to the anchor rope, expelled the water from his snorkel, and took a breath, bending forward in the water and allowing his weight to take over as he dove gracefully towards the bottom. By yawning as he went while keeping his mouth closed, he kept his eustachian tubes open and prevented his eardrums from bursting. This technique kept his hands free as he pulled himself down the anchor rope into the depths below. He had made sure, by using the tide chart, that he was in only twenty feet of water. This made it easier for him and ensured good visibility down there as he looked around to make sure everything was clear. He pulled his knife free, and because the weight belt was well-balanced, he could travel at a consistent level. He achieved his goal of finding a large clump of kelp. He didn't want to take the whole plant, so he cut off about five big leaves. His lungs were starting to tug, so he pushed off from the seabed and looked all around as he spiralled up, whistling as he went. He holstered the knife, made the surface, expelled the water from the snorkel, and made his way over to the boat. He lugged the kelp over the side and got his breath back. This time, he snorkelled over to the buoy with his license number on and followed that line down to the pot on the seabed. The half a bass was still there as bait, but otherwise, it was empty. He left it alone and again spiralled up to the surface. This time, he was more out of breath. He got over to the boat and hung on, regaining his breath. Recovered, he snorkelled over to the other buoy, dived, and followed the line down, yawning without opening his mouth to stabilise the pressure in his eardrums. As he came down to the pot, he could see the dark brown shape of a large lobster captured in the basket.

He needed to be careful and opened the end of the pot and withdrew the lobster. He felt sorry for the lobster. At least its large size showed it was near the end of its normal lifespan, and Darkly needed to eat. He spiralled up to the surface and made his way back to the boat. Darkly put his right arm over the side of the boat and gently submerged the lobster into the plastic box he had filled with seawater. He came round to the other side of the boat, took a big breath, and pushed himself down under the surface of the sea. He emerged in a column of seawater, popping up like a cork, got his torso over the side, and brought one leg up, twisting to the right. There he was, sitting in the bottom of the boat. Mask and flippers off, he returned to shore in the warmest way, by keeping his wetsuit on. As he raced over the water, he thought he reached thirty-five knots, and he was not flat-out. He was incredibly pleased with its performance.

Darkly set about getting the boat onto the trailer and parked against the fence. He transferred the lobster box to the back of the pickup, then grabbed his backpack, which contained his clothes, wallet, and soap. He dashed into the men's block, put the money in the slot, and stepped into the shower. This way, he washed the salt water off his wetsuit and himself, feeling warm and refreshed he dried and dressed. He got back to the pickup and put the top on the lobster box. He left the wetsuit in the back of the cab and set off back to the cabin. He knocked nearly thirty minutes off the journey time without the trailer, and he used less fuel as well. Good result.

As he approached the camp, he went through the gate and pulled over. Once out, he went over to the single-storey building where Larry Swartz lived with his wife.

The door opened before he could even knock, and Larry's wife came out. She was about twenty years younger than Larry, who was in his mid-fifties. His wife, on the other hand, was in her early thirties, with blond hair down to her shoulders and a well-proportioned body, maximizing its best qualities with low-cut cleavage and a hemline above the knee. Darkly also noticed a twinkle in her eye as she looked him up and down. This was the last thing he needed, as he was lying low and didn't need any attention.

He felt slightly tongue-tied as she held her delicate hand out and said, "Why, howdy now, handsome. You are a sight for a lonely lady up in these here hills. Where I come from they call me hotlips, ma Sunday name's Cheryl."

It was all he could do to keep a straight face as he shook her hand and said, "Hi, my name is Danny."

"I know. I was looking you over when you arrived."

Darkly held himself back from blurting out something along the lines of "and you all this way from Texas".

In his best-ever Montana accent, he said, "Well, Cheryl, it's like this: I've gone and caught myself a lobster, and I don't have a pan to cook it in. I wanted to share it with you if you could spare me a pan?"

"Well, honey, you come with me, and we can see if mine is going to be big enough to take what you've got?"

Darkly wondered if they could have used this as a script for the British *Carry On* films. He had to stay calm if he was going to get out of this one without laughing which would have definitely been a bad idea.

As he followed Cheryl over to their chalet, Larry Swartz came out with his usual smile.

"Oh, hiya, Danny. How you doing?"

"I'm after a pan to boil a lobster. It's going to be too big for me, so I can halve it with you, Larry."

"That's a good offer. Yeah, Cheryl will love to sort you out."

Has he read the script too? he thought. He had to remain serious.

"Hey, don't mind any of the things she says. These Texan girls don't know what they are saying, and they don't mind anyhow. Are you cooking it tonight?"

"I was going to."

"You bring it over when you've cooked it. Make a good change. Cheryl only knows how to cook steak."

He laughed loudly, which made his belly jiggle up and down. Darkly, with great relief, was at last able to laugh, and so he did. Darkly was beginning to like these two as neighbours. Cheryl came out with a pan that was big enough to hold the lobster and placed it on the kitchen table.

"There you are, big boy."

"Wow, that's a beauty."

Darkly could not help himself. He could have expressed himself in any number of less suggestive ways, but that's the way it came out. They all looked at each other and laughed out loud together.

"Take this dinner plate, honey. You can put your piece on that when you come over."

"Thanks, Cheryl. I'll bring it over when I've cooked it."

He wondered if she was going to invite him to eat with them, which he might find more difficult. He was glad to be getting away and didn't want to get into something.

When he arrived back at the cabin, he decided he had time to take his bike up the track and have a better look at the countryside. He lit the stove, placed the pan on it, and filled with sufficient water. Darkly reckoned it would be OK to leave it for half an hour or so. He took a note of the sun's height in the sky and a compass bearing.

The bike had front suspension and plenty of tread on the tyres, perfect for the track and the forest conditions up here.

As he left the campsite, it was heavily wooded on either side of the track. There was about a mile of fairly steep uphill gravel track, which led onto the ground, which was more mud, covered with pine needles and other detritus found on a forest floor. He was getting to the top of this piece of land when the trees momentarily thinned and he could see several miles farther on at a much higher level. Here, the land was even barer. He took note of this, as it meant the cover would be broken at this point and bears would be able to see him. Although he was safer on a bike, there were many areas in which a bear could outperform a human. They could run faster, swim faster, and climb trees; however, a bear could not run for any length of time, even if it could reach thirty-five miles an hour. On a bike, the main component to surviving would be to stay calm and out-think the bear. In any case, they would much prefer to avoid humans.

Darkly took note of the compass bearing of the sun and took an animal track to the right, maintaining a similar height for about one mile, then stopped. He listened to the noise of the forest; even a lack of it might give and accurate account of what was on the move. He heard the chirruping of birdsong and other noises from smaller animals as they settled in for the night. No branches being cracked or any other sounds to suggest big animals were on the move in this part of the forest. He looked at his compass again and headed straight downhill for half a mile. He took a larger path to the right and carried on across the hump of the hill, moving steadily downhill. In about fifteen minutes, he regained the track he had started on from the campsite, and he let the bike gain speed as the gravel track became firmer.

Darkly returned to the cabin and opened the door, glad to see the pan had not boiled over and was ready for the lobster. He took the lobster out of the water and pushed his knife through its skeleton behind its eyes. He really didn't like killing any animal by boiling it in water and felt it was more humane to dispatch it beforehand. The lobster was completely still now as he placed it into the pot.

CHAPTER 33

On the main floor of SIS headquarters in London, the entire team had reconvened. Several conversations were taking place at the same time. Above the noise, GHS got to his feet and asked for a bit of hush. He sat down again as soon as the din had subsided.

"I forgot to mention when we were all here a couple of days ago that Simon Knight has his own house in Pimlico."

"That's a smart move, boss. Is it a nice pad?"

"Well, yes, it is. He's a clever lad, our Simon. For one thing, he got a first in computer science and engineering. This meant he could have had his pick of officer training in any of the services. He chose the Royal Marines, opting to start at the bottom and work his way up to master sergeant and then transferred into the SBS. He was turning down any offer of officer promotion, saying all services are run by the sergeants and that was where all the fun was."

Tom Powell spoke up. "He's absolutely right. There's probably more lead flying about, but there's more action, for sure. The reputation, by the way, is that the SBS guys and dolls are tougher than the SAS."

"Well, you would say that, wouldn't you, Tom?" Sean said. "What do you think, GH?"

"I go along with what Tom says because I've heard the same. Apparently, the sea conditions in which the SBS have to train and operate make them hardier, but listen: there is a lot of competition between the SAS, the SBS, and the US Navy SEALs. Then there are the Israeli Special Forces, all very tough. Each will bring their own skills to the table. Anyway, we are not here to discuss which of these brave and wonderful services at our disposal are better than the other. Sean, if you feel comfortable starting us off with your visit to the PM?"

"Fair enough, GH. Yeah, I'm happy to start. The first post in the ground is the one to beat."

"Thanks, Sean," said GH.

"I'm not going to go on about how difficult it was to get to see our PM, Brett Caddick, or how obstructive his PA was, even though I was flashing my MI6 card around. But in the end, I got twenty minutes, and obviously, the guy has a busy schedule. My overall impression is that he is a troubled man. He appeared to be hounded in some way, unable to make the right decision about something. I got this feeling from his mannerisms, facial expressions, and hand movements. I found there had been two North Atlantic meetings between mostly Western nations. When further pressed about the agenda, he clamped up completely. He said he really couldn't tell me or my department anything about the context. He did mention that the second meeting was a lot worse than the first one. One thing did happen while I was there, and it involved the deputy PM, Peter Newton. He knocked and came into the PM's office as though he was the more senior. The reaction from the PM was that he didn't like to be interrupted suddenly, but he seemed nervous in Newton's presence. I would say their relationship was fractious."

"What do we know about deputy the PM?" asked GH.

"They often want the big job off the other guy," replied Andy.

GH said, "Exactly, although this might have gone further than that, as it looks as if there may be some sort of possible breakdown. Bear in mind, though, any further intel may well be useful."

"So, it looks like the PM has been in some way destabilised after the Atlantic meetings," said Wayne.

Sean said, "That's why Caddick looks like he has more to tell us."

Hilary was transcribing every comment onto the five whiteboards around the room, which meant that when they had finished, every shred of evidence and observation could be read by everyone in the room. That's how GH liked to run his department so that their combined knowledge became a stronger force than having individual pieces of knowledge held back by everyone.

"OK, well done, Sean. Let's crack on with all the interviews, and then we can discuss them fully at the end. However, if you have a comment in the meantime, let us know. Verity, if you would like to let us know how you got on with the deputy PM Peter Newton?"

"Get on wouldn't be the way I could possibly have put it, GH." There were laughs all around the room. They all knew from the red colour of Verity's hair that she didn't take any shit from anyone. Fit and athletic, she was extremely bright and didn't miss anything.

"I found Peter Newton a very typical political animal. Namely, he hardly answered any of the questions I asked him. I asked him why he had visited GCHQ that day, and he replied it was none of my or MI6's business. He gave me a similar answer when I asked why he had not travelled back with Simon Knight since he had taken him there. I then referred to his physical condition after the journey. He asked me if I had any record or proof that his condition was any other than normal after the journey. I did not have any proof other than word of mouth, so OK, he had me there, but it's really what he didn't say that showed he was not telling all the truth. For example, we had three people who saw he had at least a black eye. He was walking with a limp, and his wrist was bandaged, but there was no actual proof of sustained injury. I put this to him, and that's when he went ballistic and asked me who my boss was. Did he, my boss, know I was asking these impertinent questions? No question in his mind that my boss could actually have been female."

They all had great amusement at this, as Verity Hawley was a women's rights crusader. Verity laughed too.

"I then asked him if he had served in Afghanistan with Simon Knight. This question calmed him down, but he appeared to become angry at my question, as though I should not have known that. "Well," he said indignantly, "I was working with the SAS, and all their work is covered by the Official Secrets Act. I replied that the Official Secrets Act pertained to agent whereabouts and was not compromised by my asking if he was working with Simon Knight while on tour out there. This question really rattled him, and he said for me to watch out, as I was on extremely shaky ground. So, by this time, he had got me going, so I was determined not to let him off the hook. I asked him if it was true that Simon Knight had been sent on a mercy mission to rescue him, Peter Newton, from a botched and ill-thought-out foray to gain information from the Taliban by using Afghanistan interpreters, where two personnel lost their lives."

The room exploded in laughter and cries of "I wouldn't like to cross Verity."

After the general noise calmed down, Verity continued. "I have to thank the erstwhile efforts of our humble servant, Mr Thomas Powell, who provided me with amazing background intel on our Mr Nasty Newton. What a creep. Do you think I did the right thing, GH?"

"All I can say, Verity and Tom, is that I'm fucking glad you are both on our side." The room again erupted into loud laughter and this time clapping. No one was quite sure if the clapping was for Verity and Tom; GHS; or, in fact, all of them. It was a natural time to call a truce and have a mini-break.

GHS made his way over to Tom, who by this time was talking to Verity.

"That was inspiring, both of you. How the hell did you get all that intel on Newton, Tom?"

"Old contacts who are still in the navy. It wasn't hard, to be honest."

"You really nailed that little shit. I had heard he wasn't popular and that the SAS had sent him packing after that escapade," said GHS. "Let Hilary know what your conclusions were, Verity, would you please."

"OK, will do."

"Excellent," he said, nodding to both.

Everyone had resumed their concentration, and GH told them the dialogue he and Hilary had with Simon Knight's old chum at Cambridge University, Professor Paul English.

"I'll let Hilary tell you what we thought after we came out. She might have more of a female's intuition about him too."

Hilary spoke. "He was a particularly decent bloke, to be honest. He was holding back somewhat. We both felt here was where the main story was to be found. We thought, because he was very down to earth and honest in his approach to us, that gentle persuasion would be our quickest way of extracting all he knew. We felt he was holding back to protect his chum. We don't know what the real truth is behind the motives of these two, either. We will get there. Just take us to another meeting."

"To get you in the full picture here, Hilary and I may have been seen coming out of a terraced house in Pimlico last Thursday afternoon around three-thirty." A general murmur went up to the tune of "Oh yes, boss." GHS and Hilary smiled back at them.

"To quell the thoughts of those of you with nasty over productive imaginations, which I hope you all have, the house belongs to a Mr Simon Knight. He has owned it for the last twenty-seven years."

There were cries of "made-up story."

"Not at all, folks. I told you he was a clever lad. Well, guess what? He paid the mortgage off three years ago. Not a bad investment, you must agree," replied GHS.

"Is it run-down, used as a boarding house or a brothel?" asked Amanda.

Hilary replied, "No, no, it's an ordinary, beautifully decorated, well-furnished house with a bit of a garden too. Very smart. I wouldn't mind living there myself. It didn't disclose any secrets, I'm afraid. Photos of his Mother and Aunt Brenda and the three of them together. There is an album of photos of him and his buddies from training courses and action around the world, and that's in a drawer, not on display. He's been around, this guy. You could tell no one lives there permanently. It does tell us more about the man—how his mind works, perhaps. Not a drop of alcohol on the premises. GH noticed that, but you would guess he would notice that, wouldn't you?" More laughter from around the room.

Hilary quickly updated the whiteboards with what she had been saying.

GHS motioned to Andy and said, "Over to you and your friends upstairs in MI5."

"It took me some time to unravel the truth behind what they were at first willing to tell me. I had the cover that I needed to see what had happened to their computers to discover where the trouble was. Of course, there wasn't really any problem with their equipment except that theirs, like ours, had the virus. What it did mean was that I could spend as long as I wanted up there and spent the best part of a day and a half digging new bits of intel off them. In fact, I don't think they knew what I know even now. That means the door is open for me to return at will, whenever I want. The beginning starts with our good friend, the deputy PM, Peter Newton. He had been up there spreading a false rumour that Brett Caddick was about to resign. He told them he had caught him with his head in his hands, talking about taking his own life. Part of this may well have been true, at least the bit about his head in his hands and in tears. He said Simon Knight had started something and was busier than normal on the computers at Number 10. I checked into this, and it is true, but more on that later. I have to say, there is more going on in MI5 than they let on about—even to me. They definitely know more than they are readily willing to tell me. I'm not sure what, but it definitely involves Simon Knight. They really don't like our Mr Knight. What I did find out was Simon Knight had been set up by a bloke called Matt Drayson. He's the new man on the block, a rookie whose uncle is one of the big chiefs in MI5, whom you never see. They had done something together which had nearly got them all into serious trouble. They seemed to be using Simon Knight as the fall guy, and maybe they saw him as their get-out-of-gaol card. Are you all following this? It's really clear, isn't it? So much so that the word was they were trying to bump him off, especially because Peter Newton was up there digging in the knife.

What Simon Knight has done is still a mystery. Did he do something wrong, or did he do something to annoy MI5? I have yet to find out. It seems to stem from the trip he and the PM took to the *George W Bush* aircraft carrier. I didn't get access to Matt Drayson."

Sean asked, "How do you get them talking, Andy?"

"I choose a different person's computer each time. I generally find after about fifteen minutes. They forget where I'm from and are willing to let me in and drop their guard because they think it will get their computer working again. I generally find that after that time, they relax enough with me that they don't see me as a threat. I can see it in their eyes. It's Fat Andy. He's no threat to anyone. He's the computer geek."

"We love you, Andy," Amanda cried out. They all cooed.

"Hey, you know what? I don't mind one bit because it gets me access."

"That's ma boy," GHS said with a big grin on his face. "Hope you made enough sense of all that, Hilary?"

"Just about, but there's something odd going on up there in MI5, isn't there?"

"Needs a lot more investigation. Listen up, everyone. What Andy has described is exactly what this is all about. Let that intel knock about in your head. Think of all the what if's? Could it possibly be? Why are they like this? Is there a personality in there that they need to protect? Leave the ideas with you. Thanks for that, Andy, and by the way, I don't think anyone else could have got that information. Right, Tom, you went back to your friends in the navy?"

"I did, GH, and I got a journey and a half out of it. I need to clarify from the beginning that the intel I have is unsubstantiated and hearsay. Have a listen, and if there are bits that we can prove to be wrong when we've put all this together, we can change it, OK? First of all, let's talk about Simon Knight. I was able to get a lot of information straight off their own records. He had what can only be described as an exemplary unblemished record in the whole of his service—starting with the Royal Marines. As has been said before, he could have joined as an officer. Throughout his twenty-two years of active service as a marine and then in the SBS, he kept turning down requests to become an officer. He wanted the action. I won't detail all his tours, some with the SAS, but let me state clearly that he has been just about everywhere. He has an excellent degree. He's seen as smart, fit, and single—a six-feet, two-inch piece of muscle with a brain—diving, parachuting, and sea navigation tickets and still employed by the state as head of security at number 10 Downing Street. GH has already told us he paid off his mortgage, and he's still building up his pension, as he's employed by the Met now. That's smart. This next bit took quite a bit of running around, and it's probably the most important. The PM asked for Simon Knight to fly out early to check out the security and run ECMs, etcetera. Before he went, MI5 asked the PM first if Simon Knight could do some surveillance for them. The RAF flew him out in an F-35 Lightning 11. It left him there. Getting the all-clear from Mr Knight, the F-35 flew back, collected the PM, and flew him out on the same aircraft. This time, the pilot waited for the PM to finish the meeting and brought him straight back the same day. Simon Knight was on the aircraft carrier overnight and flew back the following day. How did he find his way around, you may ask? Assigned to escort duties was a Warrant Officer Jane Foster. This is her photo up on the screen, alongside Simon Knight. Both single and unattached career service people. I ask you, members of the jury, with your nasty, dirty, imaginative minds trained by SIS, to think outside the box for a moment. I ask you, could it be within the realms of reasonable behaviour that these two could have formed an international liaison? The reason I mention this is that Ms Foster has a twin brother in the US Air Force, Colour Sergeant Darren Foster, currently stationed at USAF Lakenheath. Basically, he runs the place. Why, you may ask, is this relevant? One of Darren Foster's duties is to fill jumbo flights with military personnel and cargo going to and from the States. I rest my case, m'lord."

There followed a total silence in the room as each individual came to his or her own conclusion.

After what seemed like several minutes, GH stood up, raised his voice, and in one expulsion of air and desperation, said, "Well, 'blood and sand'. Those were the worst swear words my father used.

As children, we never knew what they meant. We heard far worse out on the street, usually focussed on us black kids, but we never dared to ask him, but I use it now—advisedly."

He sat down again.

GH spoke again. "Thank you, Tom. Excellent work. What we may have is the corner of a joined-up cobweb. We have much more to do, but this may be the glimmer for which we were seeking. We will hear all the feedback before we start to form an opinion. Everyone agreed? Yes? OK, then, Wayne. If you would like to tell us about your visit to GCHQ."

"The scope of the intel I got from Colonel Grant was quite narrow. He was very helpful and didn't hold back from helping SIS. He didn't know Simon Knight, except that he knew he was head of Number 10's security. What he did say was that he had phoned Brett Caddick twice in the last month. The first time was to tell him our satellites had picked up Soviet and Chinese mobile nuclear movements—just that, at first. Incidentally, the dates of these were just after the first Atlantic meeting, called by President Ethan Miller. He also conveyed this same information to the Americans. The second phone call was to confirm more Soviet and Chinese movements and that their positions were antagonistic to our national safety and also targeting the US and many European areas. It was deadly serious intel. This, again, was conveyed to the Americans. Then, before I left, I interviewed all the staff on duty the day Peter Newton didn't travel back with Knight. Knight had spent his time in the computer room, and when he left on his own, having been told Newton didn't require him on the return journey because the message had to come through the switchboard and therefore everyone knew about it. Also—and I think this is in our interest—five minutes after Knight left, two black cars followed, full of MI5 personnel and with Newton in the second car. They were travelling away at speed. This was the afternoon that Simon Knight disappeared and Peter Newton turned up back in London with the injuries."

GHS said, "Great intel, Wayne. Thanks. Right, last but not least, Amanda, your trip to see Auntie Brenda?"

"A tidy little semi in Worcester Park. Brenda lives there alone, never married after a sister died and she took over the parenting of Simon. Retired from a teaching career. She keeps a couple of beehives, which she tends with Simon Knight, who incidentally keeps a twenty-year-old Bentley Continental in her garage under a dust sheet. She said it cost him the same as a small family saloon. I checked this out, and it's true. They go out in it when he visits—when he can, that is, about every two or three weeks, longer absenses if he's on tour. He never tells her where he's going and doesn't talk about what he's been up to. He did tell her that something big was about to happen, and the less she knew about it, the better, that he would be away and someone like me was likely to call. She did say she was more worried about what he didn't tell her than anything he had done before. I would honestly say that she knows nothing. In order to protect her, he has told her nothing. So, from our point of view, he knew something was about to hit the fan."

"Excellent, Amanda. You also visited the traffic super, Jack Hawkins. How did that go?"

Superintendent Jack Hawkins had twenty-seven years of police service. A hard man, he has seen it all. Started in the Met and moved to Oxford for the promotion. I was shown into his office by his PA. I could tell he liked me from the outset. It helped me, as he would otherwise be intimidating." Amanda read from her notes.

"Call me Jack. Sit down, Amanda. So you are with SIS, are you? Enjoying it? Work for Smithy, do you? We go back a few pages, Amanda. Good bloke. When I was in the Met, our paths often crossed. You must ask him about the bloke with one leg who dressed in a ladies bra, double D." At this, he roared with laughter.

"Could you tell me?"

"No, no, no, it's his story. It'll make you laugh. Now, what can I do you for?"

"On 17 July, you had to shut the A40 Oxford to London Road for half the day due to an RTC. We have someone of interest that we need more info about, Jack."

"Take it as read that you've seen the official police incident report?"

"Yes, and there seems to be a gap."

"Yes, quite so. You want to know what really happened, do you? Lucky you are with Smithy, because I wouldn't normally trust you. It's more than my pension's worth. Smithy and I had long chats about this sort of thing, and we came up with a routine: if anything a bit tricky occurred, we would get handwritten confidential reports for our eyes only and keep them in our own files under lock and key. That way, if it went tits up, we could always fish out the signed handwritten doc out and have proof."

He got up and went over to a small filing cabinet against the wall. Using a key off a fob, he unlocked the grey drawer, fingered through the headings, drew out a slim folder, and placed it on his desk.

"I went up there myself because there were a few dead, and the deputy PM was involved and injured. First of all, MI5 didn't want any of it to get out, so we had to cordon off the whole area and move the bodies and vehicles out fast before the press had a chance to get pictures from the air. It was obvious the deputy PM had been in a life-or-death fight. Next up, Number 10 put a restraining order on it so the press couldn't print a word. To cap that, the deputy PM didn't want to press charges against his protagonist. He wouldn't give the name, but also, it turned out he knew who it was. It was also quite clear he was carrying a sidearm, which incidentally had been discharged three times. These folders tell the story of what my officers and I saw, of exactly what we found, down to the injuries Peter Newton received to his person from the guy who gave him a right pounding. In my experience, he could have killed him, but for some reason, he decided not to." He got up, went over to the door, and ordered two teas from his PA.

"For reasons of my pension, you can read the documents but can't photo them. Nor would I want you to contact any of the officers who signed them. That's just to save my own neck, Amanda. You can't be too careful when you're dealing with these people. They are slippery fish. You can't trust them further than you could spit into a southerly Caribbean gale, as Smithy said his father used to say."

Amanda had taken the file and read through the notes. Every one was written by Jack Hawkins himself and signed off by his own officers. Amanda had made her own intensive notes as soon as she was back in her car, and it was from these that she read to the whole room and erlated everything Jack had said, especially about the one-legged man.

George Henry found it impossible to shout above the ribald remarks and laughter.

"Right, you lot. I want to put this to bed before we finish, and I'll tell you the story then. So, we've all got the whole story. We are all aware of what cracked off when the computers went down. What we need to know is why? We know where and when. We also need to know who. Hilary, would you like to put all that together after a quick break? Shout out if we've missed anything or if you remember anything extra."

They had all reconvened, and Hilary started reading off the whiteboards.

"We start with the PM appearing extremely nervous and incapable of performing his duties. Does he seem near to resignation? Is Peter Newton plotting to push him off his perch? Do we need more information from him? Then we have Peter Newton. Not the first deputy to want the top job. What was all the business with GCHQ? Was he working with MI5? Who was he in a fight with? Does it look like MI5 cleared away all the mess and cars? Did Simon Knight end up killing their operatives? Did he fight Peter Newton."

Tom asked the room, "What if the PM doesn't or can't tell Peter Newton what he has to do? Somewhere in all this, Simon Knight gets involved because we know MI5 asked him to perform a duty. Does that involve national security, something he discovered that makes them uncomfortable? Were they trying to silence him? Peter Newton would have stoked that fire, as the two don't get along."

Andy said, "What if we hang the computers going down on Paul

English? That would make sense, and if we momentarily park that idea there, we can work on other possibilities, keeping that in mind."

Amanda said, "Good idea, Andy. What were MI5 doing at GCHQ? Peter Newton got Simon Knight to take him there. Quite in order to get a lift back with somebody other than Simon Knight. Was it MI5, and if so, why? Was this prearranged? It looks that way. What were MI5 up to?"

Verity said, "Does this make our Simon Knight a public enemy? Why does it look as though he killed so many MI5 agents? No wonder he needs to disappear into thin air. What are your thoughts, George Henry?"

GH looked with benevolence at his crew. A fine lot—hardworking and good brains. They deserved his best thoughts. Psychology teaches never to answer a question. In GH's experience, it also breeds suspicion if the person directing events never takes control or allows his views to be discussed or airs a view.

"Is he still alive? He might not be. Did MI5 finish him off that afternoon? Did they then dispose of the body? I tend to think that is not the case. I think he is still alive and knew the heat was on and the safest place was far away from there. I have to admit that I veer very much between good guy and bad guy. We have quite a few facts now at our disposal. On the one hand, we seem to have an American president who wants to shut half the world down using military weapons and wants other nations to be involved. We have Simon Knight effecting the same thing using a computer virus. Question me if you don't agree, but I've got the American president, Peter Newton, and MI5 as bad guys. On the other hand, I have Auntie Brenda, Brett Caddick, GCHQ, Paul English, and the Oxfordshire Police as good guys. Where is Simon Knight in all this? We know he has a fine service record in the Royal Marines and then SBS. We know there is something hidden in all this which we have not yet unearthed. We also know that the type of work done by these special services people can play with the brains of good young men and women who never receive proper counselling when they stop killing people back on Civvy Street. Could this man, although surrounded by good guys, be behaving badly? On balance, it looks as though Simon Knight could be a good guy, but then he goes and does something against the law. I'm not ducking the question—which, of course, means I am about to—but the whole thing seems to lie in the balance. Except for one thing. We need to meet Simon Knight and see if he is willing to divulge the whole truth."

Sean said, "What about the MI5 guys he killed?"

"Could it be, Sean, that he is acting in self-defence? There were lead bullets flying around that afternoon, and they came from MI5 agents, presumably out to kill our Mr Knight. He's too well-trained for them, too bright, too skilled. Instead of the two carloads of MI5 agents getting their man—and don't forget someone, sent them to do this—they came up against what we have come to expect from our special services, be they Royal Marines, SAS, or SBS. Not only that, but we have Peter Newton, who also seems out to kill our Simon Knight. Who is pressing his buttons? And to cap it all off, Knight decides to draw a line and spare him his life. What is that all about?"

The whole room started talking together. GH decided this really was what he wanted.

"We can reconvene in two hours—talk, argue with each other, throw ideas around. I think we need to find this guy somehow. Two hours."

GH and Hilary left the room together and headed downstairs for some fresh air. They came out into the street noise on one side and the Thames on the other. The old river, green and brown, passed by at over six knots. As they stood still and took in all the noise of the river traffic, it seemed fast-flowing, wise, and knowing. Many oaths had been shouted across it, and many truths too. So much going on. Would it help with their own quest for the truth? It had already. GH took off his coat and turned his face towards the breeze. The sun's rays made him feel good. He turned to Hilary, who had been his companion on many of his escapades in SIS.

"What do you think, Hils?"

"You always say, 'Think like the other guy.' He needs to get to somewhere remote. Where did he train? It would be near the coast, somewhere he wouldn't attract attention or where there was no one there to begin with."

"Yes, some of their training at the beginning is land-based and with the SAS. The Brecon Beacons is one area. In reality, it's not big enough for a long stay, and also, how would you find food? I think your first thought was closer to the mark. I would tool up with a boat, and given my water skills, I would live mostly off the sea. Where would we go?"

"Europe's out. Too busy. Plus, he's more likely to stand out. Same for Eastern Soviet or ex-Soviet territory and the Baltic and Nordic states," said Hilary.

"Africa—you could get lost in Africa. Get ripped off or murdered too."

"South America?"

"Definitely a possibility."

Hilary said, "North America. What's the difference between the East and West Coast, GH?"

"East is more temperate—cooler in summer and hotter in the winter. Hotter the farther south. Probably more fish farther north."

"In Australia, although it is English-speaking, I think you would stick out more."

"Agreed. So, realistically, we are left with North or South America. Again, I think South America would offer too many risks. For example, whom could you trust? Could you get done over? Could you go and buy a boat? What's the possibility of criminality?"

"So, does our money go on North America?"

GH said, "I think that's our answer. So now, how do we get there?"

"No idea."

"The answer could come from Tom's picture."

"What do you mean, the girl?"

GH said, "Seems to be his only contact with the opposite sex. Doesn't have any obvious male friends. He is popular with his old muckers but often doesn't turn up to functions. Maybe too busy with work. Would you like some ice cream before we start back, Hils?"

"Yes, GH, and it's my turn. You got them last time."

GH and Hilary strolled into the big room, still eating their ice cream cones.

"Oh, look, the privileges of senior management."

GH laughed. "You have got to learn where the best food is to get on here, Sean."

"I've had to put up with Verity's awful tea-making."

"OK, next tea-making course, Verity's on it."

"Oh, boss, I made him coffee anyway." Verity looked at Sean, stuck her head in the air, and shook it from side to side in a mock tantrum. Sean laughed, as did his colleagues.

"OK, guys and dolls, serious stuff now. Get your choices of hideaway on bits of paper and say how many of you were on that team. No names."

Hilary took back the sheets she had handed out and read the results. "We have one for Scotland, one for South America, and five for North America, including Canada."

"Wales? Nil point, eh? Yes, although he trained there, it's difficult to hide. Like Scotland, it's good for the short term but not for the long term. Hilary and I also looked at South America. We thought if he knew someone who lived there, it might be possible. He may have someone from the services, but that's unlikely, although we haven't checked, so keep that in mind. North America as a whole, then. The more borders he has to cross, the more risk. So, if he landed in the States, then that's where he is. We all need to be very fluid with our thinking. For example, if you disagree, please feel free to follow your gut feeling, and try to make a case for that. Any ideas as to how he would get to America?"

The ideas and crossing of thoughts carried on for another two hours.

"There's no obvious way for him to get to America without us picking the movement up on our surveillance. We had all the airports, ferries, trains, and busses, and we had the roads blocked off for three hours."

GH said, "Yes, fair enough. We need to get back to our contacts and dig out more information on this guy Simon Knight. It really looks like he is our felon, and we need to catch him and get him behind bars before he kills anyone else. A couple of thoughts. Does he have a private pilot's license? Does he have any friends with boats? How does he get around London, for example? Is there something we don't know yet? He has his Bentley in Worcester Park. We know that is still there—thank you, Amanda. Are there any other little nuggets hidden in the cupboard we need to find out about? Off you all go, and we'll meet back here in twenty-four hours. Is that OK for everyone?"

They all agreed and went back to their preferred partners they were with before.

GH and Hilary headed back to Pimlico Road to have another search around.

They entered the house through the back door, their entry point, before using GH's set of lock pickers, which he carried on jobs like this. They started at the top of the house and methodically worked their way down to the kitchen. Finally, they found the key cabinet, which was situated at the top of the cellar stairs, in front of the locked door to the cellar itself. They had torches and used these to make their way into the three rooms that made up the cellar itself. In one room, the floor had been covered in rubber matting, and it housed a bench press with single- and double-handed bars for a selection of weights. An elliptical bike occupied one corner, and in the other corner, a solid bar had been cemented into the brickwork, obviously for pull-ups. Suspended from a ceiling joist was a boxing punch bag, and to one side was a small table with 14-oz boxing gloves and an egg timer.

"All you need in here to keep right up to peak fitness, I would think," said GH to Hilary, who was impressed with the basic set-up. The other two rooms had been dry lined to guard against dampness. One was used as a store for all sorts of bits, and the other gave them a shock.

There was a workbench along one wall with a bicycle stand, and beside it, there were puncture-repair materials and numerous wrenches and spanners. One drawer was reserved for spare inner tubes. On the top of the set of drawers was a lubrication gun and the typical three-on-one oil can. The larger of the drawers had a selection for bicycle chains.

Hilary said, "So, we unearth an unknown. The man's a keen cyclist. How interesting."

"Yes, after the fight with MI5, if he had his cycle with him, where could he have got to, keeping in mind he avoided the main roads? This might provide a helpful clue to where he went and how he vanished into thin air. The trouble is, if he used his bike, where did it take him? We have time to get to Cambridge—if that's OK with you?"

"Ooh, yes, I wouldn't want to miss that part. We may get a bit closer, do you think?"

"I do."

CHAPTER 34

It took them one and a half hours to get out of town and park in the university car park. The traffic hadn't returned after the business had faltered following the massive computer breakdown over the entire country, if not the world. Governments were playing down the whole thing, of course, treating their paymasters, the people, like idiots and pretending it had not been as bad as it was.

"Hello, Professor. How are you?"

"*Apprehensive* is the way I would express my present mood, Mr Smith."

"I can understand that, Professor. Tell me all you know. I need the truth, or this could turn very ugly for the pair of you."

"What do you want from me, Mr Smith?"

"Right, well, I need to know where Simon knight is. I need to know how to get rid of this virus you designed."

"The honest, simple answer is I honestly don't know where Simon is. He felt the only safe way for those of us involved would be to know nothing. The virus has been simply designed and has a simple function, namely, it is impossible to enter any computer that has this virus in it. There is no trigger to open the computer so that even the most sophisticated antivirus mechanism could retrieve anything from its memory. The computer might need replacing or at the very least at least a new hard drive. I must point out that as far as we were concerned, the US had organised a huge nuclear bomb strike. Many, many millions were about to lose their lives. The effects from nuclear pollution, winds, and fallout— these sorts of thing, which remain unknown—could devastate the earth for years. Of course, I wasn't factoring in the nuclear threat. You were acting on your own suspicions. You performed no research to back up the tapes. They could have been a practical joke for all you knew."

"Absolutely not, GH. You may remember that when Simon came to me the very first time, I asked for a week to think about it. Well, what I did was hack into the research data in the United States, and guess what I found: the figures were all correct. That much was true. What he had got the scientists to do was deliberately use the wrong algorithms and move the timeline forward by a matter of two hundred years."

"You mean this is going to happen anyway, Professor?"

"Yes, most scientists in this field would agree that we have two to three hundred years. If, by that time, we have not made changes to the way we live and addressed the issue of overpopulation, something like the president described may occur. This information is itself top secret. If the general public worldwide had access to these figures, you can only imagine the mayhem which would occur. Just think what it would be like if Joe Public thought his entire family was about to be wiped out in six months would he even go to work again?"

"I have to say, Professor, this is a lot to take in. My mind is blown apart. It is exceedingly difficult to listen to what you are saying without identifying as a human being."

Paul England stood up and walked towards a map on the wall behind GH and Hilary.

"When I first came across this information, I was knocked over. I had no one to tell. I decided not to share this new data with Simon, as he would never have achieved what he did. I started to sketch the areas highlighted for the bombing on this world map. I worked out the size of a nuclear bomb to encompass that area. I then drew red circles to delineate the affected areas. It really did leave me speechless. I was as shocked as you two obviously are. I also had to calculate that the figures the president gave to his fellow world leaders were false. He, therefore, had an ulterior motive for presenting them. A reasonable assumption would be world power and trade domination.

After wiping out all his major manufacturing competitors, he would be able to rule the world, as well as send the United States' GDP through the roof. I had one chance to prevent this from happening: make the virus as virulent as possible. I have no apology for that, GH. I must also point out that I have a wife and three children, I really enjoy going to work, I have a decent salary and pension, and I might be swapping all that for years rotting in jail."

"That, Professor, is out of my hands. The fact that you have been helpful will work in your favour. We have to get back to London. We will be in touch."

CHAPTER 35

Communication was starting to get easier, and some forms of transportation were returning. Power was also becoming available, and other basic functions were showing signs of returning to normal. GH, however, had a noticeably big problem on his hands. They had a half-day meeting, from which they were all exhausted. They had thrown around all the intel they had collected and knocked around all their ideas. Simon Knight—was he a demon or saviour of the world? The main sticking point in his mind was whether to put all his eggs in one basket and bank on the fact he had gone to the States. Should he look at other options or aim for North America? Was he confident he had gotten deep enough into Simon Knight's mind that he was sure he knew his whereabouts?

Fortunately, he slept well that night, probably because he was exhausted. As he woke up and swung his legs out of bed, it came to him in a flash. It was obvious. No sooner had his feet hit the carpet beside his bed than his idea formed into a plan.

He arrived at work and stated the strategy to put his plan into action.

"Tom, you and I are going to Lakenheath."

Tom said, "When are we going? I thought you might be interested in our Sergeant Foster."

"Precisely so, Dr Watson." Tom could see he was in a buoyant mood. Something must have triggered this.

"What I want you to do this morning for me, Tom, is use your charm and contacts in the services to get us an hour with Sergeant

Foster. He is not in any trouble; I just need to talk to him. I do not want any trouble with his superiors. Explain who we are, and explain that we need some information from him—that is all. One little thing I would like this afternoon."

"Wow. That may be difficult, but I will do what I can."

"As quickly as you can. Thanks, Tom."

CHAPTER 36

Darkly woke with the birdsong. This morning, he was spending some time down on the coast in the semi-rigid. He threw some clothes on and took some money to buy groceries and some snap for lunch, which he would probably take on the water. He washed his face and brushed his teeth, and as he was opening the driver door of the Ford, his mobile rang.

"Darkly, it's Jane. Honey, I love you like there's no tomorrow. I'm Longing to touch you again."

"Hi, Jane. It's great to hear from you, sweetheart. I guess I'm in trouble?"

"Difficult to tell. Let me tell you the full story. Are you OK to talk?"

"Carry on, Jane."

"Yesterday afternoon, Darren had a visit from the head of your SIS—Smith, George Smith. Said he was on your case but not to panic. Seemed to know exactly how you got to leave the country."

"Darren's not in any trouble, is he?"

"No, not at all, apparently. Smith calmed his worries and said he had done nothing wrong. Just said he wanted the truth."

"It didn't take them long."

"Yeah, but they don't actually know where you are, you know. Darren reckons they were stabbing in the dark. He was caught because he didn't want to compromise himself in case they came back to question him again."

"He did right, Jane. You must assure him he did the right thing. What did he say?"

"Well, it's surprising how much he got right. For example, he said you had turned up on a bicycle? How the hell did he know that? He also knew you were headed for the States."

Darkly said, "It's all about getting inside the other person's head. What would you do in his position and with his experience? Have you heard the expression, 'Walk a mile in the other guy's shoes'?"

"Oh, yes, but I hadn't really thought about how to use it."

Darkly said, "Neat little trick because I now have to get in Smith's head. So, let me guess: he told Darren I'm not necessarily in any trouble and to come back and talk to him?"

"In a nutshell, yes."

"I had to kill four MI5 people and nearly took out the deputy prime minister, and I'm not in any trouble? You see, Jane, why I can't trust what he is saying? It's a ploy to get me back in the UK, as they don't want to put out an extradition order; this would attract too much interest on both sides of the pond. That is the last thing they want."

"Do you say coat and dagger?"

"It's cloak and dagger, Jane. I love you."

"Over here, we would say it's underhanded and shoot them in the chest."

They both laughed, and Jane told Darkly she loved him to bits and back.

"Anyway, to continue, Darren said Smith was a broad-shouldered black man with great presence, with eyes that drilled straight through you. He finally had this message. I've been instructed to write it down." Jane paused here, and Darkly could hear the rustle of paper. "'Revelations 6: Satan shall come from heaven imitating the coming of Christ, also riding a white horse.' Smith doesn't know if you are Satan or saviour. Is this how British cops talk, Darkly?"

"Jane, there is a message in there somewhere, and I still would not trust him farther than I could throw him."

"Sounds like even with your strength, you wouldn't throw him very far, Darkly."

Darkly laughed so hard he was barely able to reply. "I need to be careful, Jane. So yes, I will return, but on my terms."

"What do you mean, Darkly?"

"They won't know when or where or how. Was there a reply number for you to get back to him?"

"Yup, Darren has that number."

"Tell Smith I'm Kalki riding the white horse. That's K-A-L-K-I."

"OK, got that. No idea what you're talking about."

"In Hindu mythology, Kalki was a saviour who rode a white horse. I won't know whether they agree until I face the music back home, will I?"

"Guess not. Hey, when do I get to see you again, you big hunk?"

Darkly explained he had previously researched the planning for his return, and it would take him over five weeks. The less Jane knew, the safer. Darkly told Jane to get rid of the sim card in that phone and ditch it. He said he would contact her as soon as he could and not to worry. She implored him to stay safe. They voiced their love for each other, and the line went dead. Darkly was alone again.

As he had previously planned, he emailed ten shipping companies as Simon Knight and applied to their adverts for second navigation officer posts because that position was better for his scope of experience, and all his navigation certificates obtained during his time with the SBS were in his own name.

He started the pickup and made for the coast. The journey was spectacular. As he came down off the mountain range, the land became greener, and before long, the ocean came onto view, which was a dazzling sight and one which he would miss. He had enjoyed his time here and could have stuck it out a lot longer.

He entered the car park and was immediately confronted with a crowd of people, some with yellow jackets and some in typical coastal gear, standing around the jetty. A large motorboat had been backed down the jetty; its nearside wheels had gone over the side, and the trailer had become stuck when its chassis had crunched down onto the concrete of the slope. This had dropped that side of the trailer to make a thirty-degree angle, and it was stuck fast. The lorry pulling the trailer was perhaps big enough to pull the trailer back onto the slipway; however, every time they tried to bring the trailer back up the jetty and get the wheels back onto solid ground instead of hanging in mid-air, the boat took a more severe angle, as the trailer slewed further to the right because it was resting on the axle, which was angled downwards.

Darkly made his way over to the commotion. Jeff was in a serious conversation with a man who appeared to be the owner, given he was the one with the reddest face and looked the most stressed (stressed being an understatement).

Jeff was saying, "I think we are going to have to lift the boat, Mr Hooper. Don't think there is another way."

"A crane to get here is going to cost me a fortune. I ain't got that sort of money, and the insurance won't touch it, the bastards."

"Jeff, can I have a word, please?"

"Danny, hi. Look, I'm a bit tied up here for the moment."

Darkly firmly took his elbow and steered him out of earshot of Mr Hooper. Jeff looked at him as if to say, *What the hell are you doing?* Darkly leaned across and said into his ear, "How far is the fire department from here, Jeff?"

"Why are you asking that, Danny?"

"Do you know anyone there?"

"Sure. Went to school with Carl, the fire chief."

"OK, here's a plan. You know the air balloons they use to lift trucks back onto their wheels when they have been involved in an accident?"

"Yeah, know what you mean."

"Call Carl and see if he would like to do an exercise here, right now. Then, if we positioned the airbag up against the jetty and under the wheels and put a sleeper or two on top of it as it inflated, it might put the wheels back up to the height of the jetty, and if the truck driver let one of the fire crew pull his rig forward—so we know it is going to be done right—we would be back in business at no cost."

Before Darkly could turn around, Jeff was already on the phone calling his mate Carl. Darkly went over to Mr Hooper and, in an even manner, told him to calm down. Jeff had come up with a plan. He briefly went over it, and even before he had finished, sirens could be heard making their way through the afternoon traffic towards the harbour.

A tiller truck was the first to arrive. Next came two bright red engines. The first one made its way over to the jetty side. It kept well to the right of the truck attached to the boat trailer. As it stopped, the crew sprang onto action, and six men opened cabinets in the side and hauled a black airbag out onto a heavy canvass sheet with rope hand grabs. They grabbed the hand grabs and hauled the sheet over to the edge of the jetty and down onto the sandy beach below. While they were doing this, another of the crews had taken a petrol engine compressor out of the third fire engine's side cupboards and wheeled it to a position above the bag, still out of the way of the truck. They unfurled a reinforced hose from the compressor to the bag and, once it was connected, started the engine, and the bag started to inflate. A couple of sleepers appeared and were placed on top of the bag under the wheels and held in place by two of the crew. All this time, Carl, the fire chief, had been quietly directing his team. As the sleepers on the bag rose and came into contact with the wheels of the trailer, the weight kept the bag in place, and as if by magic, the wheels of the trailer were lifted higher and higher until they had reached the level of the jetty. The motorboat had become level again and had stabilised. The compressor was stopped, and once again, the fire chief quietly and confidently instructed the driver of the tiller truck, which had been the first to arrive, to hop into the truck's cab and start to pull it forward. The boat trailer moved slowly forward as the crowd clapped and the first wheel rolled up and onto the concrete of the jetty amid cheers from the crowd.

Jeff walked across to where Darkly was standing and shook his hand. "I owe you one, buddy. Thanks a million."

"No problem, Jeff. I'm off out on the water myself for a couple of hours. Will you be around when I get back?"

"Yes, this will take me another hour to sort out. I'll look out for you returning. Good one, Danny."

Darkly went over and prepped his boat, connected the trailer, backed it down the jetty, and slipped it into the water. He tied it off and took his rig away from all the commotion, then parked. He walked across to the semi-rigid, jumped aboard and started the engine, untied the painter, and reversed out into the deeper water. He took the gearshift out of reverse and pushed it forward, then made his way out of the harbour area. As he passed over the bar, he pushed the throttle forward as far as it would go. The sea was flat calm, and the boat cut through the water under full power. As this might be his last journey, he meant to enjoy it to the fullest.

When he had made it to his lobster pots, each contained one. He pulled them into the boat, as he had to clear the site if he was not returning. The lobsters were transferred to the box filled with seawater. He had tied their pincers so they would not hurt each other. As he started the engine for the last time, he had a sad feeling about leaving this area that had given him safety and a good place to hide. He pushed the boat to full speed for the last time and enjoyed the sea wind in his face and the taste of salt on his lips. He thought of Jane and what the future might bring them and whether he could remain safe. The fantastic turquoise colour of the sea when it was tranquil, as it was today, made the journey back to the jetty even more poignant. Still, it was better to get back and face the music. This Smith guy was MI6 or SIS. He had a good reputation, and the reference to the white horse might have meant he saw there had been good from the work he and Paul had done. He could not trust him, though. He had to play it doubly safe.

Jeff was waiting for him as he finally approached the jetty.

"Hi. I saw you coming over the bar, so I made my way around."

Darkly tied the boat off and jumped out onto the concrete.

"I'm afraid I won't be staying as long as I wanted, Jeff. Things have changed back home, which means I have to return straight away."

"Nothing bad, I hope. I've watched you control this semi-rigid, and you know what you're doing. Your handling skills are very impressive."

"That's the thing: I need to sell the whole rig, Jeff. I wondered if you might be interested."

"Wow, the trouble is I would love to, but it's the cost for something like this. It would probably be too much for the kitty right now. I have to report to the local council, and they are as tight as a camel's arse in a sandstorm, Danny."

"It might help that I bought it well off a bloke inland near the lakes who had no use for it. What would you expect to pay for it, Jeff?"

Jeff explained, giving Darkly a figure that rigs like this would fetch in season.

"I know I can't afford anywhere near that."

"Halve it and then take 20 per cent off it. That would be around what I need, Jeff."

"Jeez, you for real? I might be able to swing that, Danny. I can call the head of the council. He is in business and knows the value of the rigs we have here. I've discussed many times the need for me to have a better craft. It would bring in more money, too, because I could get out when the weather's bad and patrol the whole estuary. Give me five minutes, Danny."

This gave Darkly the time to get the boat onto the trailer and out of the water. He was cleaned up and had everything in place. He was moving the lobsters out of the boat when Jeff returned.

"I don't know how to thank you, Danny. You saved my bacon earlier with Mr Hooper, and now you've fixed me up with a boat that will help me do my job better and easier. Yes, he says that's a good deal and I can spend that money."

Jeff shook Darkly's hand and gave him a big smile.

"That's great, Jeff. Think you're going to like the deal even more because I've got two lobsters here and can only handle one of them."

"You're kidding me, Danny. You some sort of saviour, Danny?"

"I hope so, Jeff. I hope so." Darkly smiled to himself.

Jeff came over and gave him a bear hug. "My wife loves lobster, and there are very few around this time of year. Wait until I show her this and tell her today's story. Shame you can't meet her." Jeff looked down at the ground. "We would have liked that."

"Maybe I'll be around next year, Jeff. I'll try to come back. After all, Montana's not that far, and I've really enjoyed my stay. I owe you my thanks."

"You know, Danny. Maybe we have been good for each other. Over the year, I've been worried about how I can keep on top of my job using my old boat. I've got the cash in the harbour office. By the way, if you give me fifteen minutes, you come along, and suddenly my problems are solved. You even let me have the credit for solving today's accident, and I get a lobster to take home. Buddy, you will always be in my mind."

Darkly had rarely been complimented so much, and it brought a lump to his throat. He had only been doing what he had been trained to do. His mind went straight back to early days when he had joined the marines, where he and the other new recruits had been told their job was solving problems and helping other people by sea or land. He gave a couple of kindly pats to Jeff's shoulder, nodded, and turned towards the pickup. Within a very short time, Jeff was back with the cash. He thanked Darkly again. Darkly turned and opened the Ford's door, climbed in, started it up, and drove away, giving Jeff a wave.

He did feel Astoria had, in some way, saved his life. Smith may have been smart and lucky to have worked out how he could have gotten to the States. It would have taken another six months to have gotten even close to finding out where he was, though.

It was what it was, and he needed to move on. He got glimpses of the coast as he climbed up into the mountains and drove over the tops and on towards the cabin and campsite.

He pulled in and stopped just as Larry and Cheryl were coming out of the front door to their bungalow, heading towards their four-by-four Jeep. They were dressed smartly, and Larry was carrying a bag. Cheryl looked for all the world as if she was going to start a night shift as a hostess in a nightclub or even a casino. Her yellow blouse had sequins all over and was low cut, and her black skirt was short, and with high heels. She looked a dream.

Larry gave Darkly a wave and said, "Did you need us, Danny?"

"I've got another lobster, Larry. I was after borrowing your pan again if you would like half."

"We are off out, Danny. Going to stay with a couple of old friends of ours overnight."

Cheryl had gone back into the bungalow and appeared with the pan. She put her forefinger on Darkly's chest and said, "Here you are, big boy. There's some tin foil to wrap it in when it's cooked. Pop it in the fridge, and we can eat it cold tomorrow. Here's the key. You can leave it under the pot at the side of the drainpipe over there," she said, sliding her finger across his chest and pointing to the potted plant in question.

Darkly thanked them and wished them a happy evening, once again holding back his laughter. He realised they were well-meaning and kindly people, if a little eccentric. They drove off with waves, and Cheryl blew kisses at him. A few years earlier, he might have gone bright red. It would have been tricky to tell them out of the blue that he was leaving first thing in the morning and he had decided he would leave them a note when he took the lobster over later that night. He had paid upfront for six months, and it had been such a good place to drop onto. He was pleased that Larry was four months up on the deal. He had, after all, been able to sell his boat, which had been a plus. He was also going to be a bit cheeky and use their washing machine to catch up on his dirty laundry before he left.

Darkly set about starting a fire in the log burner. He gathered up anything that might benefit from a wash and made his way back to Larry and Cheryl's bungalow, making sure he didn't drop a sock on the way in. He searched out their washing machine. It was in a small utility at the back. Easy to operate, and there were tablets and conditioner on the top. He went back to prepare his lobster, and this time, had bought a Thermidor sauce to go with it, along with some salad. He had also got provisions and plenty of fruit for his journey over the next few days. It would make it easier, especially as he didn't have Jane's conversation and company to keep him awake over the miles ahead. He nipped back to transfer his washing to the tumble dryer and wrote a long note explaining that unfortunately things beyond his control had changed and he needed to return. He thanked them both for making him feel at home, then collected his clothes before he got back and finally cooked the lobster. The sauce complemented the lobster's flesh, and he thought it was the best he had tasted during his months there. As he allowed their half to cool, he packed what he could and laid everything out for the morning.

He walked back with theirs half wrapped in the tin foil in the pot they had lent him. The evenings were starting to get lighter, and although there was a nip in the air, it was pleasant to have the whole place to himself and listen to all the animals prepare for spring. The birds had started to forage as they looked for more food to improve their plumage, ready to attract a mate, make a nest, lay eggs, and feed the young—a process that took every bit of energy from them every single year. *And we as humans grumble*, he thought.

He delivered the foil package to the fridge and left the cleaned pot on the table next to the note he had written the night before. He collected his dry clothes, locked the door, put the key in its place, and enjoyed his walk back in near darkness. Once he had slipped into his sleeping bag, he was sound asleep in one minute.

CHAPTER 37

He woke with the birdsong, ready to start a new chapter in his life, which he knew he had to face to move on. How would he be received? He could not trust the message in the white horse, Satan or saviour remark. It was most likely bait to entice him back. He couldn't do anything about it now anyway—it was do or die. He had a clear conscience concerning his motives. He had to face it at some time, and if he stayed away any longer, it would only put the people he left behind under higher scrutiny. He threw some bread and cheese down his throat, finished the last of the milk, had a shave and brushed his teeth, had a bucket shower, and put on his fresh clothes. After a final tidy-up of the chalet, he took his bike out and put it in the back of the pickup and locked up. On his way past Larry and Cheryl's bungalow, he dropped his key off along with their key and got back on the road, heading east.

He kept the sun behind him initially. Then the road led him south, with the sun on his right shoulder, and after about an hour, he turned left again, with the sun behind him as he kept on the high road on top of the mountains as he headed towards the Oregon-Idaho border and dropped down into the valley. He kept following the valley road as it wound its way south and westwards. It was marked as the Snake River Plain. The pickup was an easy vehicle to drive, a large, powerful engine coupled with an automatic gearbox. A high sitting position made for easy motoring, and it gave him time to dream a little. He couldn't help thinking about the early settlers and the indigenous population, their fight to keep the land, which they farmed sustainably. They initially fought with bows and arrows against the rifles and lead bullets of the incomers. The same way the empires of history had been won time and again—by the British, for example. He reflected on the sadness and death from the outcome of the arrogance and aggression to take more territory and have greater wealth.

He turned off right and headed back up the mountains toward Salt Lake City. He crossed into Utah, and an hour later, he was heading east again, entering Wyoming. This was another treat for him, as he was back up in the Rockies. Every corner brought him views that took his breath away. The road took him through Rock Springs and on towards Medicine Bow Mountains and through Cheyenne. His knowledge of native Americans was patchy, but he recognised that name—the Battle of Little Big Horn, where Custer of the US Army fought against them. There was a notice to say that Cheyenne meant "Like-Hearted People".

I don't think it worked out well for the Like-Hearted People, he thought as he headed ever further east, with Denver well to the south. He was dropping down again as he crossed into Nebraska. The scenery changed, and it was obviously a big farming state—different farms of all sizes, mostly arable, as it had the most fertile and productive soil in the States, good for crops as well as grazing. Some of the farms stretched for miles and miles. He had travelled one thousand miles, the light was starting to fade, and he felt tired. He pulled into a motel and booked in. Fetching some food from a diner, he ate in his room. He showered, and as soon as he hit the pillow, he went straight to sleep.

In the morning, he ate, filled up with diesel, and carried on towards Omaha. Around mid-day, he crossed the state line into Iowa, heading east towards Chicago, which he hoped to make in the day. He stopped at a roadside diner to clean up, bought some food and coffee, and ate on the move. It kept him awake and alert. He went over and over his plans once he had completed his navigation spell on the container ship. Landing in the UK was going to be a vastly different game. He would be the hunted once again, and he needed to use all his skills not to be arrested or worse. Would they be out for a nice, easy elimination, with no loose ends and untidy questions? He really couldn't be sure, and he wasn't going to trust Smith until he had met and assessed him. He drove on and on at a steady sixty-five, able to watch the sun moving around the pickup as the day progressed. He stopped again as he crossed into Illinois, had a decent meal, and decided to get more miles on the clock before passing Chicago. He passed south of the city and again caught sight of Lake Michigan. It looked like a sea, and again, he wanted to go north and have a look at Milwaukee. He knew it could be a dangerous city, but it also had parts that were OK to visit. Also, he could cycle around. He would see what Jane would say if he was ever free to be with her in the future.

He was now in Indiana, and it was only a couple of hours before he crossed the state border into Ohio and reached Toledo. He pulled into a service area, filled up with gas, and took a meal. He chose a motel and again crashed out for the night. He knew he had about nine hours of travelling the last day before reaching New York port, where his container was moored, and before signing on for the crossing, he needed to sell the pickup.

As Darkly woke up, he read the email he had received from Ocean Shipping Lines, the US-owned company he would work for on the *Oceanic Blue* container ship, destination Immingham, UK. The captain was Athos Kadmos. The first officer, to whom he was to report, was Otto Samuelsson. Twenty-seven thousand TEU, report 1100 hours in three days.

He acknowledged the email to say he would be there and requested permission to take his bike on board. He set off with the sun on his back. He wanted to arrive in the free port area of New York that same day, which would give him time to sell the pickup and get into gear for the next leg of the journey.

CHAPTER 38

The whole office was present and ready to discuss the demise, or otherwise, of Mr Simon Knight.

GHS asked the room if anyone wanted to start the proceedings.

Tom Powell spoke first. "As ex-services, even though the guy seems genuine and mostly ahead of the game, he has killed four MI5 operatives who were on official government business, as far as we know."

Hilary looked at him and said, "I consider that MI5 was being played along by Peter Newton to benefit himself and his ambition, by giving them misinformation. This led to the slaughter on the A40, when Knight was ambushed and outnumbered and came out on top."

Verity spoke up in support of Tom. "This bloke should not be let off the hook. He had no authorisation to do what he did, and he acted outside his brief. What the hell did all this cost us all in the end?"

Andy spoke up. "I'm on the fence here. I know the cost to our computer system. What if all the countries who were affected sued us for the damage and loss of earnings? We would be broke and looking like fools."

Wayne agreed with him. Being the oldest team member at fifty-six, he said he wouldn't be surprised if they never saw Knight again and his body was never found. That might have been the simplest solution, anyway.

Amanda disagreed. "Not at all. What if he's a hero and saved millions of lives? Personally, having met his aunt, I believe he is a good guy trying to do the best thing in a hostile and corrupt environment. His bad press comes from people I would not trust, like Peter Newton and William Hassop-Greene."

Sean spoke. "Seems to me the fella was being attacked, but he was well-trained and fought back. He won and escaped, realising he would be liquidated at a moment's notice. He had a plan to disappear. We now know that was to the States. If the boss hadn't come up with a solution, I doubt we would have found him in the next six months or more. I also think, as Amanda does, that, in reality, he helped to save millions of lives of innocent adults and children. I would say let's see what he does next so that we see how he reacts."

GH took over the meeting again and said, "We have a few different ideas. We will get to the right answer. Stay calm, think it all through, and also learn. If your idea of all this is different from the final truth, that's OK. Your voice is still valuable while you are learning from the process. I have a bigger responsibility in this situation, and so, I have to wait until I meet him to be able to judge him. You may find this attitude frustrating and think I am not answering your question. I see a few of you have discussed the final answer. I have also had a meeting with the PM early this morning to keep him up to speed with where we are. Between us, we decided to interview Mr Knight in front of me, the foreign secretary, the home secretary, and the PM himself. MI5 has not been included at the PM's request, as he is in the process of a complete restructuring and has been mindful of the necessity of this for some time. This may also give you a clue as to where we are probably going on this. Bear in mind, we may be proved wrong yet."

Hilary asked, "Do we have any idea how he might contact us and whether he is on his way?"

GH spoke. "We already have the normal means of arriving covered between us, and I know there is no movement, as I have heard nothing from any of you. Try to get inside his head. First, he doesn't know or trust us. When he breaks cover, he will have an escape plan in case things go wrong for him. His arrival will be a surprise. Therefore, if we expect that, we may be able to handle it better. So, if we have a sighting of a canoeist with a pushbike strapped on and paddling towards the bank, it's him!"

They all broke into laughter. "Incidentally, if he has underwater gear on and backflips into the water, which way would he travel?"

Tom shouted out above the uproar, "Downstream, boss."

"Correct answer," GH shouted back. As the laughter subsided, GH quietly took Hilary to one side and said into her ear, "Actually, it's quite possible."

CHAPTER 39

Athos Kadmos, captain of the container *Ocean Blue*, leaned over to pick up the ringing phone. "Hello, Simon?"

"Docking in fifteen minutes, Athos. Port authorities have offered us Eimskip Warehousing, two miles from the main port. Reduce knots to three, and the pilot will be on board in five—repeat, five—minutes."

"That's fine for us. Thanks, Simon. I'll take over on the bridge from here. When you have a moment, I would like a word, please."

This was the sort of thing that sent Darkly's fear response into overdrive. Was the pilot the only officer to come on board? Where could he go if they somehow predicted his movements? Best to get it sorted. He got up and told the first officer, Otto Samuelsson, a wonderfully spoken Swede with whom he had got with very well.

The Eimskip was a secure docking area where they used their own stacker to offload the containers, and it was the quickest method. Immingham dealt with 46 million tons of cargo annually, which made it the largest in the UK. The dock was a town in itself, quite a massive sight of sea, lights, ships, and movement, working twenty-four hours.

Darkly entered the bridge and stood beside the captain, who took him to one side to talk in his ear. Athos, a gentle Greek from Athens with a deep, highly accented voice, said, "I know you signed on for Immingham, but when we finish here, we now have seventy-two containers to load for London docks. I don't know your plans. Simon, would you like to stay on till then?"

"Yes, Athos. That would be fine, thanks."

"More pay, my friend." He laughed and patted his back pocket. That would work even better for Darkly—much better.

He had a plan for the journey from Immingham to London, but this played right into his hands, and he was happy to take up Athos's offer. He had got on with the captain and the first officer, Otto. His cabin was comfortable, and the food was OK. It also allowed him more time to plan his final meeting with George Henry Smith.

The trip down the North Sea was uneventful, with routine navigation into the mouth of the Thames and on towards the Isle of Dogs, where they would dock and unload straight onto a rail system, a rapid method of unloading. Darkly said his farewells and collected his bike, and once his helmet was strapped on, he became invisible among all the other Londoners who rode the town on two wheels and found it the quickest way to get around. His first job was to find accommodation, where they were least likely to find him. How cautious should he be? Would they be out looking for him, or had they decided to let him come to them? There was no way he could know. Caution would be the only way forward.

CHAPTER 40

GH Smith's desk phone rang.

"It's Simon Knight. I'm here in London, and I'll be in touch for a meet within the next six hours." The phone went dead.

Peter Newtons phone rang. "We think we have him coming west on Whitechapel, boss. Computer picked up his bike and cycling gear from previous surveillance months ago."

"OK, get the van and pick him up. Take him to the safehouse we spoke about last week."

"Will do. I'll make contact once we have the cargo on board."

Darkly was cycling towards the South Place Hotel, an upmarket hotel in EC2. This would be the last place they would expect him to hide: right under their noses.

He had heard the vehicle behind him, and the next moment, an arm went around his neck. Another had his bike, and together, they were hauled into the side of a moving van. The door slid shut, and his hands were cuffed. They yanked his helmet off him and replaced it with a hood. No one spoke as he was thrown about in the back, and within ten minutes, the van had drawn up and reversed through what sounded like a tunnel, which would have been between terraced houses to gain access to the rear. The engine was turned off, the side door slid open, and he was pulled to his feet and held in a crouched position beside the van. This was followed by three hard blows to his stomach and a fourth punch, an uppercut to the face. He felt the unmistakable cold steel of a gun muzzle pressed to his temple.

"Try anything, and it's over for you, Knight." He was dragged along a short yard through a door, along a corridor. There was a sharp turn to the right and down some steep stone steps, into a cellar which smelt of damp. He was pushed down hard onto a chair, which didn't move, and Darkly knew it must have been fixed to the floor. His lower legs were tied together and bound to the chair. His legs and his elbows pulled harshly towards each other behind the back of the chair, which would have hurt his wrists if he hadn't tensioned them before they tied them off. There were three sets of footsteps up the stone stairs, and the door at the top was shut and locked. Darkness and silence.

Round one to them, he thought. The uppercut to his face only glanced off his cheek—not a good hit. One guy was short, and the other was not as tall as him. The third he could not tell and may have been the driver. Was this MI5 out for revenge? Was Newton involved? He knew he would have a contact somehow. They had nothing to get out of him and gained nothing to keep him alive. They would torture him and then kill him was his best guess—out to sea and over the side, never to be seen again.

Shit.

Smith knew he was here in London, but there would be no way to find him, and he would not be missed for at least another four hours. *No cavalry. You're on your own, Darkly*, he thought. *Keep thinking. Make a plan.* The first would be a soft beating. The second would be broken bones, and the third, he did not want to contemplate. He needed to make a move early, while he was still strong.

Darkly kept going over and over in his head how he would achieve the best result with the least risk. It must have been about three hours before two sets of steps came down the stairs.

"I need a shit," Darkly said.

"You can fuck off."

"Well, if you want shit flying about all over the place, it's up to you, but I need a shit. Now."

The third voice came from the top of the stairs. "I don't want his shit all over the place. Bring him up. He can use the one up on the first floor."

They undid his ankles and elbows and manhandled him up the first flight, along the corridor, and up the second. It was difficult, as Darkly couldn't move easily. He was thrown onto the toilet, and the door was left ajar. "I don't want to watch the bastard crapping," one said to the other.

Darkly quickly whipped his hood off and started fingering his collar. He found the pin and went to work on the handcuff lock, first bending and working the pin until he could feel the click. He quickly leaned down and undid the rope binding his legs.

"Get on with it, you bastard. One minute."

He didn't need a minute. He took hold of the door and gently opened it enough to see out. The taller of the two was farther up the landing, and the other was leaning on the frame of the toilet door. Darkly made a small noise, causing the guard leaning on the frame to spin round and receive a terrific blow to his jaw from his handcuff-bound fists. In an uppercut motion, he broke his lower jaw in two, and his teeth flew out of his mouth as if he had suddenly coughed while eating a mouthful of nuts. He hit the floor unconscious. Before the taller second abductor could move, Darkly took one huge stride. As he already had his hands holding the cuffs high in the air, he brought them swinging diagonally down hard into the man's temple, and he went down with hardly a cry for help. Darkly frisked them for weapons and took a knife from one and a Glock 17 from the other. He checked to ensure it was loaded—you never knew what imbeciles were like—and made for the stairs. As he got to the top of the landing, a bullet whizzed up through some of the woodwork and spindles of the staircase and landed in the wall.

Darkly had already taken the safety catch off and aimed downwards and low. The driver went down with a cry of pain as his kneecap exploded and blood splashed all over the wall. Darkly thundered down the stairs three at a time, giving the guy who was bent down holding his injury a soft kick in the face. It sent him reeling, unbalanced onto his back. Darkly stood on his left arm and, with his free hand, held his head away from him, towards the wall.

192

With one knee on his chest and the Glock 17 held over his wound, he said, "Who are you all working for?"

"Fuck off. You can go and get stuffed."

Darkly dug the Glock into his wound and twisted it around.

"You bastard, never. Ahhhhhh."

He dug it deeper into the wound, and the man arched up into the air as the pain nearly rendered him unconscious.

"Now, I'll ask you nicely one more time: Who are you working for?"

"No, no, don't. I can't. Ahhhhhhhhh." Darkly pressed harder, then released the barrel, and the man's torso floated down onto the carpet once again. "I told you to fuck off."

"So you did." Darkly dug the barrel into the wound again, working half the guy's patella to one side with a deep grinding sound.

"Newton."

Darkly clubbed him unconscious. He frisked him and found the keys to the van. He raced up the stairs and dragged both the men down the stairs and into the cellar. He went up again and brought the last one down. Working for the SBS meant that knots came as second nature. He tied a noose around each of their necks, then their hands to their feet and both ends of the rope to the static chair. He raced up the stairs and out into a small yard, closed the side door, and started the engine. He came out slowly onto the street and headed east, taking note of the house number and street, keeping the Thames on his left. He pulled into the first parking space and again phoned Smith.

He explained what had happened and the connection to Peter Newton and the number and street name of the house.

"What's the reg on the van, first of all? Then, I want you to leave it, and I'll get Scotland Yard to pick it up. Change your clothing colour, and put your helmet on. Start walking eastward along the embankment with your bike. A silver-grey people carrier, reg number PR 2 M, will pick you up and take you to safety. I will meet you tonight, along with some others, and we will listen to your full story and take it from there."

Darkly noticed the people carrier as it slowed down and stopped.

A blond man of about thirty, broad and well-muscled, jumped out and came round, opening the side door.

"Simon Knight? I'm Tom Powell. I'm from SIS. Mr Smith said I would find you here."

"Hi, yes, I'm Simon."

"Jump aboard, Simon, and we can put your bike in the row behind you." It was a marvel to him that he still had his bike with him. Within two hours, they had swung through brick pillar gate posts with their pointed spikes, and at the end of the drive sat the impressive sight of Chequers, the PM's country residence. Built originally in the mid-sixteenth century, it was bequeathed to the nation expressly for British prime ministers who might not have had the wherewithal to own a country estate and needed to relax or entertain foreign visitors after the First World War.

In the meantime, GH had organised Scotland yard to track down the MI5 safehouse, apprehend the three, and find out who they were and their story. He had already alerted the PM to set up Chequers and been up to question William Hassop Greene. He had then, at short notice, invited Graham Bennett, the foreign secretary, to join him and the PM for the evening.

Darkly was shown through the huge front door and into the hall. The tall ceilings, carvings, and ornate furnishings were impressive and well-appointed. He was certain he had a great deal of blood on his clothing and face. Darkly became aware of his surroundings and the state he was in and what he must have liked. He was dirty and needed a long shower desperately. Darkly pulled out a paper handkerchief and started to wipe away some of the grime. The older man, showing him the way, turned to him and said, "You don't need to do that here, sir. You'll find things very relaxed, friendly, and informal. Your room has an en suite with a bath too. We're going straight up there now, sir, and you can take your time to freshen up. I'm informed your fellow guests will be at least three hours." He led the way up the galleried staircase to the first floor and along a wide corridor, carpeted with a deep, sumptuous pile.

"I was also told you may be in need of fresh clothes, and if you aren't offended, I'll get you an informal outfit, all brand new so you don't have to worry. My name's Harry. I'll fetch them up to your room and pop them just inside the door."

"Thanks, Harry. That would be very kind of you. As you can see, I've had a bit of a day so far."

"I'm here to make your stay as pleasant as possible. If you need me or want to ask anything, press nine on your room phone, and it will come straight through to my mobile, OK?"

"Great, Harry. Thanks very much."

Harry used a key to open the door to Darkly's bedroom. He handed him the key and gently closed the door behind him as he went.

Darkly phoned Jane. She picked up immediately.

"Darkly, is that you?"

"Yes, I'm safely back in the UK. How are you?"

"All the better to hear you and know you are safe."

"I'm good, Jane. I've really missed you so much. I look forward to seeing you again."

"When would that be, as I've been saving my leave so I can see you, just in case you somehow survived?"

"I could say come straight over, but I don't know yet what is going to happen to me. I have a meeting tonight, and I should have a good idea after that."

"Can we talk now, or do I have to wait?"

"I'm covered in blood at the moment and need to clean up. When are you free tomorrow?"

"Oh, Darkly, you do make me worry. Are you OK? Are you injured?"

"Jane, I honestly haven't got a scratch, but you should see the other guys."

"You haven't been killing more people, have you, Darkly?"

"No, I needed these scumbags alive to vouch for the truth."

"Thank goodness for small mercies. Phone me first thing your time, Darkly. Is that OK?"

"Definitely. Speak to you in the morning. I love you."

"Love you too."

Darkly dialled a number into the phone. "Good afternoon. Brenda Bennett speaking."

"Hi, Auntie B. It's Simon."

"Oh, Simon, let me just sit down. I'm all of a flummox. Right, where are you? When are you? How are you? Why did you?"

"Well, I can answer some of those, perhaps not in that order, though. First of all, I'm back in Blighty."

"Oh, good, dear. And?"

"I'm unharmed."

"Oh, good dear. And?"

"I'll ring you tomorrow. Full explanation, promise."

"Oh, good, dear. You know, since your …"

The phone went dead. Darkly put it down and contemplated his future. He didn't have any clue about tonight. It could go either way. He had decided to tell Auntie B as little as he could; otherwise, she would worry. He decided to shower and spend time making himself as presentable as possible, even in borrowed clothes.

While he was showering, Harry knocked and left his new clothes on the chair by the door. They fitted OK, and Darkly dressed and rang Harry's number.

"Yes, sir."

"Simon, please."

"How long have we got before the others arrive, do you know?"

"About an hour, I would say, from what I was told earlier."

"In that time, would it be in order for you to show me around the place?"

"That Simon is entirely within my realm. When would you like to start?"

"Well, Harry, I'm ready now, if that's convenient with you."

"I will be there in five minutes, Simon."

In five minutes, there was a knock at the door. Darkly opened it and followed Harry down the corridor and down the main staircase into the hall through which he first entered. Many of the rooms had chequered floor tiles, which impressed him—the detail monied people of the pre-1920 era would take to impress their visitors. There was a beautiful indoor swimming pool that led to manicured gardens. Many areas had seats for different groups to enjoy or discuss politics or do whatever they wanted. Inside, the furnishings were sumptuous and not at all faded, and there were plenty of colours.

There was the Hawtry Room, where Winston Churchill broadcasted many of his wartime speeches. There was a splendid library with a great selection of books. There didn't seem to be any contemporary editions. He was sure there would have been some, but they were not easy to find. Darkly was fascinated by the Long Room and the countless Oliver Cromwell memorabilia. The room contained jaw-dropping artefacts. The main dining room was large enough to seat thirty to forty people, maybe more. The ceiling had carvings, and the ambience was overwhelming. Past the dining room lay the drawing room, where in days past, only the gentlemen would withdraw to drink their brandy and smoke their cigars.

CHAPTER 41

GH sat on the right of Brett Caddick, with Graham Bennett to his left. In front of them, Simon Knight looked uncomfortable.

Brett Caddick spoke to Darkly. "Why don't we start from the meeting we had in Number 10, when I told you we were going out to the North Atlantic and that MI5 wanted a word upstairs."

Darkly spoke. "I went up to one of the smaller offices upstairs and met Matt Drayson from MI5. He told me they had a new silicon listening device, which Brett had cleared for me to use, and they wanted me to conduct a trial at a meeting. They said it couldn't be detected with any of the latest devices; even the American scanners would not be able to pick it up. So, considering that Brett had, as far as he said, sanctioned it, I thought that the obvious place to trial it was the meeting that Brett was going to as we would be able to know if the Americans would be able to pick it up. That part went really well, as the solution had been installed into a pair of reading glasses I could wear into the meeting room onboard the USS *George W Bush* aircraft carrier. It was easy to squeeze the solution under a table during my initial checking of the room for devices, and it set in sixty seconds and would pick up any sound and yet switch off when it was quiet. It would record about one and a half hours of sound. I collected it the day following the meeting and arranged to meet Matt Drayson, who wanted me to listen to the recording to give my opinion of its quality and whether I had hit any snags installing and harvesting it later."

Graham Bennett asked Darkly, "What was the meeting about, may I ask, which then prompted you to act outside the law, which is presumably why you are here? All I know is that the lights went out and none of the computers around the world worked for about four weeks. Was that your doing, Knight?"

Brett Caddick stepped in. "Graham, for security reasons, there is knowledge about the whole of this affair that has been kept from you and many others—for your own safety, at least in the immediate future."

"What on earth are you talking about, and why am I here if you can't give me all the facts?"

"Would you agree, GH, that we let Simon carry on and fill Graham in later on any of the details, of which he will be unaware at the moment?"

GH said, "I agree, Brett." He turned to Graham Bennett and said, "The whole story is quite convoluted and intense. If we let Knight carry on, Brett and I can fill you in later. Bear with us."

Darkly carried on, "The initial research from the States' findings that the earth's temperature would start increasing unless we stopped polluting the atmosphere immediately, within six months and then increase exponentially until within twelve months the temperature would be at a level that human life would be unsustainable."

Graham Bennett, who was normally a thoughtful, measured man, jumped up and raised his voice. "What? You made this up, Knight. It can't possibly be correct."

Brett Caddick interjected, "It is what Ethan Miller would have had us all believe. It later transpired that the scientific data had been falsified and brought forward by two centuries, but we didn't know that at the time. Carry on, Simon."

Darkly battled on, knowing from the look on their faces that he had an uphill battle. "At the end of the first North Atlantic meeting, the US president said he wanted a vote on all the countries using military weapons to bomb a huge number of countries in the Southern Hemisphere to take out either innocent populations or manufacturing areas, China being the major target."

Graham Bennett again raised his voice. "You have to be making this all up, Knight?"

"Not at all, Graham," Brett Caddick said. "The whole conference was in a complete uproar, as you can imagine."

Graham Bennett bristled. "Huh, if you say so, Brett. I'm having difficulty believing anything he says. But go on, indulge me." Graham Bennett added, "How the fuck did you get all this information, Knight?"

Darkly started, "Listening to the tape was the last thing I expected to happen, to be honest. I collected the silicon device by peeling it off the underside of the table. I put it in the little box Matt Drayson had provided and brought it back to the UK. The next day, when I had arranged to meet him, it was Matt who suggested I listen in and comment on what I thought of the quality of the recording. At this point, there was no indication at all of the dynamite it held."

GH asked, "What did you do next, Simon?"

"I really didn't know what to do, but I did need to discuss what I had heard with the one person I could trust, and that is my best buddy, Paul English."

GH said, "Paul English is the professor of computer science at Cambridge University, which is where Simon met him, and they have been close friends ever since."

"At this point, we knew nothing about the nuclear proposal from Ethan Miller."

Graham Bennett was on his feet again, starting to go a shade of puce. "Come on now. I think we've had quite enough of this nonsense to know that this madman needs locking up—and we need to throw away the key."

Brett Caddick interjected, "Please, Graham, we need to hear the whole of this story before any judgement is made. Carry on, Simon."

Darkly started again, "I discussed the climate change with Paul, and we both thought the evidence might be wrong, for a start. Secondly, we thought about the military threat and agreed that it brought new sinister thinking into the equation. In the meantime, MI5 took me to one side and threatened me with my life if I didn't keep quiet about the tape and started to watch my every move and bugged my house. Brett then told me there was a second meeting and that he needed me again. Before we went out to the North Atlantic, Matt made contact and asked what developments there were? I knew MI5 watched my every move and there was going to be no way to go without them finding out."

GH spoke. "Why didn't you go to Brett at that time?"

Darkly replied, "I thought MI5 must have known about the meetings to contact me when they did, so either they had been told by Brett or they had someone on the inside."

"I definitely didn't tell anyone about. Wait a minute. I remember that I was in horrible mental trauma after the first meeting. Having to shoulder the information on my own made me want to vomit. I was spiralling into depression, and I felt very low, thinking I couldn't carry on. Peter Newton caught me being sick in my office one night. This caught me off guard. Until this moment, I had totally forgotten that I had told him anything. That's quite bizarre."

"So, if he knew then, who was his contact at MI5?" asked Graham Bennett.

"In his position, there is only one answer: William Hassop-Greene." GH suggested.

Graham Bennett tapped into his phone and almost immediately came back with, "They were at the same public school together, the same year."

Brett Caddick said, "That may be the connection. The cunning fox—I never did trust him. There was always something sneaky about him, my wife said. She is never wrong. I received a message that I need to be back in London tonight, which means I have to leave but will be back first thing in the morning. We can reconvene then. I can be back by eight-thirty tomorrow."

"I have to get back too and will see you all then," said GH.

Graham Bennett said it would be OK with him, and in any case, he would like to run over a few things with Simon Knight.

"I get the fact that you took the silicon listening device with you to the next meeting, but why didn't you discuss that with Brett?"

"Well, first of all, it was a bit last minute, and there wasn't time or opportunity. It's really only in retrospect that we can judge the seriousness of the portents of the meeting that we can understand that it should have been handled differently. I thought that Brett knew what they were going to throw at me. It was only after I had listened to the tape that I needed to have another viewpoint, which was when I contacted Paul."

"Why then didn't you go back to Brett?"

"After MI5 threatened me, I thought I couldn't trust anyone. I also knew that at the drop of a hat, I could be eliminated."

"Then, amazingly, you decided to go it alone with Paul English?"

"It didn't happen like that at all. After the first meeting, it hadn't been obvious that Ethan Miller was going to use nuclear."

"Your story is maybe starting to fall into place. What I still don't understand is why you two chose to activate a devastating virus, intending to do so much damage to so many different functions of our lives, businesses, and government facilities—including our military—and you went ahead without a second opinion?"

"It didn't really start like that. I originally went to see Paul because I could trust his integrity—and also to offload this awful dilemma I had found myself in. The idea of the virus didn't crop up until the second meeting. We didn't know who to go to for advice. It was only after the second tape that Paul had come up with using a computer virus to stop them going ahead with the nuclear solution."

"We will obviously have to discuss your behaviour fully and decide what to do with you. Are you staying here for the night?"

Darkly answered that he was and that it was an order rather than a choice. Graham Bennet got up and departed.

Darkly couldn't pick up whether the guy was onside or not, but then, he had never had much to do with his big bushy eyebrows and piercing green eyes before.

He seemed to be the sort of politician who was excitable and would also get things done.

When he looked up, Harry was entering the room where they had held the meeting.

"How are we, Simon? I've been told you are here for the night?"

"Yes, that's correct, I'm here under orders, although I do like it; it's a lovely house to stay in."

"Yes, we are used to getting unusual visitors under unusual circumstances, so don't feel we are not used to it. Where would you like your meal tonight?"

"What are the choices, Harry?"

"Easy, really. I can lay you a table down here, or I can bring it up to your room. There aren't any other guests here tonight, and the PM's not in residence."

"It's getting reasonably late, Harry, so I'll eat in my room, thanks."

As soon as Darkly was back in his room, the phone rang.

"Simon, it's George Henry. Are you free to talk?"

"Go ahead, GH."

"Just want to update you as to where we are. The Yard visited the address you gave me and took in the three for questioning. One of them did have to go into St George's casualty before they questioned him. Thankfully, he and one of the others sang like canaries; they didn't want the blame for something that had nothing to do with them. It boiled down to the fact they were not going to take the can for their boss at MI5. So, William Hassop-Greene was brought in too, and he also sang like a canary. This then put the spotlight on Peter Newton. He was brought in and is currently being questioned, but he is not saying a word."

"Blimey. So, maybe there's light at the end of the tunnel?"

"Well, it does look like it, although they don't hold out any hope for the truth from Peter Newton."

"So what happens next?"

"Tomorrow morning, you will be joined by Paul English. I will be there, as well as the PM. Stay where you are, and I will see you in the morning."

"Thanks, GH."

The line went dead as there was a knock at his door. His tray was delivered by Harry.

"Here's the food you ordered, Simon. Will you need anything else?"

"No, I'm happy, thanks. Do you ever get off duty, Harry?"

"I'm off now, and I'll bring you your breakfast at seven-thirty in the morning. Sometimes it's like this, and then we have quiet spells, so the job evens itself out in the long term."

"Thanks again, Harry, and for showing me around earlier."

"Pleasure, Simon."

The following morning, Paul English joined Darkly at ten o'clock.

"Are we in terrible trouble, Simon? I'm really worried."

"I wish I had more to tell you, Paul."

"I'm worried about our freedom. Will they want to impose sentences on us. What about the kids? What about my career? And never mind my marriage. I feel like weeping. I haven't slept for nights. It's been terrible."

"Hold it together, Paul. The picture is not as bad as you think. First of all, there is the deputy PM skulking around with his own agenda to overturn Brett Caddick."

"Isn't he the one you pulled out of a nasty situation in Afghanistan?"

"The same. He is being interrogated at Scotland Yard at this very moment. Probably our biggest card—if they don't want any of this to get out. I think they will try to keep it quiet because of the embarrassment that the two of us were able to cause such a massive problem."

"What do you think our chances really are, Simon?"

"Sixty/forty."

"You have always been the more optimistic. I'm afraid I'm on the forty, and we go down."

"When you think about what we avoided and cleaned the earth up. I'm the only one who actually stepped over the line."

"Can't help thinking we are in the shit, Simon."

They heard voices and looked around to see Brett Caddick and GH striding towards them. They settled themselves around the table and ordered more coffee.

GH opened proceedings by introducing themselves.

"You two gentlemen are in hot water. We are aware from conversations with Simon here that you devised a computer virus that caused mayhem worldwide, which cost a huge amount of money. Simon here, on the other hand, also caused several deaths before he chose to disappear to the States.

Have you anything to add, Paul?"

"Well, I-I-I mean … we didn't mean." At this point, Paul English felt his throat completely dry up, and he started to cough and wheeze and hyperventilate, clutching himself around the neck as he felt he was going to collapse.

Brett Caddick was on his feet in a flash. He put his hand on Paul English's back, gave it a tap, stretched over to the table, and picked up a fresh glass of water.

"Dear, man, we aren't here to hang, draw, and quarter you. Keep as calm as you can. Take deep breaths. That's it—hold it in and breathe out as slowly as you can."

At this show of unexpected kindness, Paul English convulsed in a fit of sobbing while trying to apologise at the same time.

"I never realised it would work as well as it did. It was only meant to knock out the nuclear strike." He sobbed.

Brett Caddick said, "Look, you both did me a big favour. I could not possibly have pressed the button. I think it would only be fair to let you know how we are going to deal with this. First of all, we need to know whether either of you has told anyone else about what has happened?"

Darkly said, "No one on my side, Brett."

Paul English blurted out that he had not told a soul.

"Not even your wife, Paul?" GH asked.

Gaining a little bit more control over his emotions, Paul English replied, "No, not even my wife. Wow, if she had found out what I was up to, I would have been hanged, drawn, and quartered." They all laughed, which took the heat out of the meeting, and they were able to carry on with more ease.

"What about your Aunt Simon?" asked GH.

"Honestly, same as Paul. I couldn't afford to tell anyone."

Brett Caddick continued, "OK, that's good. You both crossed boundaries you shouldn't have. Luckily for us, no one has been able to put the massive computer malfunctions at our door. We need to keep it that way. You will both have to sign an edited document of the Secrets Act 1989, which will put you in jeopardy of confinement if you defer to it. We cannot afford to let this out of the bag. In that way, you are both very lucky. Peter Newton didn't know all the facts. He has been asked to stand down as a member of Parliament and put on a retirement plan and cannot take part in any further public duties. William Hassop-Green is similar and has been stripped of public office in his lifetime. Other measures, which I won't go into, have been taken to ensure we have complete confidentially on the whole matter. Paul, you can report back to work and carry on as normal. You will be watched from time to time, but rest assured you are lucky. Simon, tomorrow morning you are to meet GH at SIS HQ and receive further instructions."

"Got that, Brett, and thanks."

Brett Caddick said, "It may well be that our thanks are due to you both, but I'm afraid we won't be able to show you."

Brett Caddick and GH said that a courier would arrive in the next half hour with dispatch boxes containing their documents to sign. These would be taken straight back to Brett in Downing Street once signed you will be free to go. They got up and left the room.

Paul looked at Darkly and smiled. "Sorry. I behaved like a turd, didn't I?"

"You, my lovely friend, are not used to any of this web of intrigue and backstabbing I got you involved in. We, on the other hand, are all used to this type of stress. So, get back to Cambridge, enjoy your freedom and your students and family, and I will visit just as soon as I am able. It looks like I'm in the clear—except that they obviously have something in mind for me to tackle."

They hugged, and Paul said, "Tell you what, Simon: I'm on my way home with a lighter heart than the one I came with."

"That's a good end to the story, Paul."

Darkly watched him go and marvelled at his fortune for having such a friend. He was also elated by the way things had turned out for him.

Darkly made his way up to his room, entered, and packed his bag. There was a knock at the door, and Harry entered.

"Simon, we have a car to get you back to London."

"Brilliant, Harry. I'm all packed and ready."

"Was it a good stay, Simon?"

"Harry, I can't say it wasn't interesting, but it's a great place to work, isn't it?"

"Yes, it is. May I ask, was the ending a good one for you?"

"A lot better than some I had envisaged, Harry. Thanks."

"Well, I'm glad, Simon."

Darkly followed Harry along the corridors of portraits, busts of famous people, and the sheer history of the place, which couldn't help but impress any visitor, down the impressive staircase. He crossed the courtyard to his waiting car. Harry placed his very unimpressive suitcase in the boot.

"It's been good to meet you, Harry."

"Likewise, Simon, oh yes before I forget your bikes already been put in the car."

"Thanks Harry, you've looked after me very well."

Would MI5 hold a grudge against him? Their boss had been removed, and the whole department had been reshuffled, and maybe the new MI5 didn't know who he was. Peter Newton had been barred from government and quietly given what amounted to a suspended sentence, so he shouldn't give him any more grief. He might as well sit back and enjoy the journey, and at least when he went into his own home, it wasn't going to be bugged, and he would be able to relax.

He had done all the things when you have been away from home for some time. He had cycled down to the local shops and restocked the provisions he needed to keep him going for a few weeks, done a general clean over, changed his bed linen, put a stew in the oven, thrown in a jacket potato, and was sorting through the mail that invariably mounted up inside the front door. Darkly was very comfortable in his front room armchair. His phone rang.

"Hi, Simon. It's Darren Foster."

"Hello, Darren. How are you?"

"I've a bit of good news for you. Jane will shortly be boarding a United States airline bound for Lakenheath. I have a few days off and will be bringing her down to London sometime tomorrow afternoon. Do you have parking on your street?"

"Wow, that's a great surprise, and yes, I have a parking permit that I never use, and it's in date."

"That's perfect for me. I have a meeting first thing and will be free in the afternoon. Are you coming straight to the house?"

"Yeah, that is my intention, buddy."

I'll see you tomorrow then. Hey, that's brilliant news. Thanks."

In the morning, Darkly cycled down to SIS HQ, and with some trepidation, he gave his name to the efficient-looking man on reception.

"Mr Smith is expecting you, sir. He says he will come down to meet you himself. If you would like to take a seat, he says he won't be long."

Darkly thanked him and went to find a position where he could see as many entrances and exits as possible. *Old habits die hard*, he mused.

George Henry Smith swiftly yet quietly worked his through the reception area, followed by a neatly dressed woman, wearing a knee-length dress and blond shoulder-length hair, which swung from side to side as she walked. She carried an air with her, which gave her the appearance she would not tolerate being messed about.

"Morning, Simon. Good to see you. This is Hilary Payne, my PA."

They all shook hands, and Darkly nodded at Hilary. She met his gaze and gave him the faintest of smiles.

"I've booked a room at this level for our meeting if you would like to follow us, please."

They took a door out of the back of the reception area, and for such a grand building with such a high-end architectural style, the corridors were very plain and like many new builds in London. They eventually turned into a medium open-plan office, in full view of the other offices, as all the walls were made of glass.

GH started and said that Hilary had a burning question which she would like answering.

Hilary spoke to Darkly. "When you left the Oxford area, having been ambushed, what were your motives for disappearing to the States?"

"Yes, it may have looked like I was jumping off the drowning ship into the burning sea. Do you know what happened at Oxford, Hilary?"

"You were ambushed by five MI5 personnel and the deputy PM. The latter kept his life, and you dispatched the others, in addition to wrecking three cars and a farm gate. Does that cover it?"

"I had formed a plan as an escape in case things went wrong. I had already been threatened by MI5 and knew some of the people chasing me. I had already completed my task—"

Hilary interrupted him. "What exactly was your task?"

"To plant and install the virus Paul had developed to stop the military on all sides from starting a full-scale nuclear war. The States wanted to take out large areas of the manufacturing world as well as other larger areas of overpopulation in order to ease a forthcoming climate change catastrophe. China and the Soviets were teaming together to defend China from this attack."

"So, why did you want to disappear to the States?"

"I didn't feel safe here. When I was ambushed, as you put it, I knew MI5 was out to eliminate me. My strategy changed that afternoon to one of defence. My only choice was to use a predetermined escape plan I had been able to put together in case of trouble."

"OK, I get that."

GH asked Darkly if he knew why he would be asked to SIS HQ. Darkly replied that he had no idea?"

"Well, we have a job for you working under me and using Hilary as your main contact. Would you be happy with that?"

"I don't know either of you well enough to know I would be happy. What would the job entail?"

"The prime minister knows you reasonably well and likes the way he work. Since he has been PM, he has noticed large amounts of money being earmarked for different high profile jobs, and then when followed up six months later, the money and trail of it has disappeared completely. He thinks that in the past, the pressures of previous holders of his office have not had the time to take enough notice, and it has gone unchallenged. The idea would be that you work in total isolation and secrecy undercover to find the route that this money, which has been earmarked and put to one side until it disappears. The intel would suggest there are civil servants working with MP's through designated banks to move the money around so that it can't be found and that it is eventually divided around and making these individuals extremely rich, which in itself makes them even more powerful."

"Shit, that sounds like one hell of a task."

"It is. We want to use your computer science degree to place you in positions where over time, you could monitor money transactions being deposited in the bank accounts where you are working. Once we have a picture of the movements and possibly the people involved, we can remove you and take over and move officially. That way, we can keep using you under different covers to settle similar business elsewhere. These people will be very powerful and cautious and suspicious, as well as dangerous, Simon. Do you think you could handle something like that?"

"I would have to have time to think it over. I would guess I don't have too many options."

"We don't want to blackmail you into doing this. You need to be happy to perform at this level. I don't think you will have any problem thinking on your feet and getting out of trouble, should it be necessary. Brett has seen the way you operate, and the pair of you get along well. This work could also carry on after his term in office has finished."

"Would I have the same salary and pension?"

Hilary answered, "Your salary would increase by two grades, as you would be on the same tier as our operatives, which is higher than your grade was at Downing Street. You will also have an expense account which we can talk about later. Your pension would be commensurate with your start date, with no loss of service. As you know, you were paid throughout your stay in the US."

GH said, "You will be part of our team here at SIS HQ. When you've had a couple of weeks off, I would like you to come in and meet the whole team."

"I would be happy to meet everyone. Thanks, GH—and of course, I have already briefly met Tom."

"Thanks are also due to Brett Caddick. He wanted someone special to head this one up, and you turned out to fit the requirement. You will deal directly with Hilary here. No one other than Hilary, me, and the PM will know any of this for the moment at least."

Darkly left the building and took a deep breath in and looked at the greenish-blue of the Thames and knew he had made it home safely. Quite how, he was still unsure, but here he was, safe and in a new job which excited and interested him.

He opened his front door and felt for the first time for a long time that no one was looking over his shoulder. The house needed a quick once-over. He decided to shop first and then get on with the dusting and hoovering. It wouldn't take long as he had very little ornaments or mementoes of his youth, as any that there were had remained at Auntie B's.

He busied himself getting everything clean and tidy and was absorbed in the detail of that when the doorbell rang.

He opened the front door, and there, right in front of him, was Jane, looking so beautiful with Darren holding her case behind her. They flung themselves into each other's arms and held each other tight.

Darren said, "Are you letting us in, or do I have to stand out here on the street looking like a lame duck until it goes dark?"

"Sorry, Darren. I didn't mean to be rude. Come in. I've got loads to tell you."

Jane looked at him and said, "I'll bet you have."

La Fin

Printed in Great Britain
by Amazon

84688823R00130